"Let me take you to lunch, if you don't have any plans."

Kendra's heart beat faster. Her mouth felt dry as she stared into his warm eyes. "Sure. Why? Did you want to go over the appearances scheduled for next week?"

"No, I'd like to talk about us. I know you asked me not to." He countered her objection before she could make it. "And while I respect your feelings, I don't believe you're being honest about how you feel or what you want."

Nate cupped her face in his strong hand, lifting her chin so her eyes met his.

Kendra backed up until her back pressed against the wall. Her heart beat so quickly she was sure he could hear it. She stared at him, unable to speak. Her chest was heavy with all the things she wanted to say, and her head was spinning, reminding her of all the reasons she shouldn't say them.

He captured her mouth in a kiss. Slow and sweet. Filled with warmth, affection and desire. Her hands slipped beneath his jacket, pressing into his back. Her body softened against his.

Dear Reader,

Reading *Pride and Prejudice* by Jane Austen as a young girl changed my life. It ignited a desire to weave stories that make readers laugh, cry and swoon.

Elements of that story subconsciously weave themselves into the fabric of every story I write. Unconventional heroines, family drama, crises of self-identity, the revealing of devastating secrets—all are present in my Pleasure Cove series.

The Johnstons and Williamses—two polar-opposite families—lie at the heart of the series.

In *Playing with Temptation*, we become intimately acquainted with both families. Passionate and driven—on and off the football field—Nate Johnston's propensity for unfiltered honesty jeopardizes his future, forcing him to entrust that future to the woman who destroyed it seven years ago—his ex, Kendra Williams.

Enjoy your visit to Pleasure Cove. Then, for series news, reader giveaways and more, visit reeseryan.com.

Happy reading,

Reese Ryan

Playing

WITH

Temptation

REESE RYAN

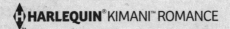
HARLEQUIN® KIMANI™ ROMANCE

Recycling programs
for this product may
not exist in your area.

ISBN-13: 978-0-373-86508-6

Playing with Temptation

Printed in U.S.A.

HHARLEQUIN®
TM www.Harlequin.com

Reese Ryan writes sexy, contemporary romance featuring colorful characters and sinfully sweet romances. She challenges her heroines with family and career drama, reformed bad boys, revealed secrets and the occasional identity crisis, but always rewards them with a well-earned happy ending.

A native of The Land (Cleveland, Ohio), Reese resides in North Carolina, where she carefully treads the line between being a Southerner and a Yankee, despite her insistence on calling soda "pop." She gauges her progress by the number of "bless your lil' hearts" she receives each week. She is currently down to two.

Reese is an avid reader with a to-be-read stack that resembles a small skyscraper, and a music lover with a serious thing for brilliant singer/songwriters and an incurable addiction to Broadway soundtracks and film scores. Connect with Reese via Instagram, Facebook or reeseryan.com.

Books by Reese Ryan

Harlequin Kimani Romance

Playing with Desire
Playing with Temptation

Dedicated to self-sacrificing single mothers
like my mother and paternal grandmother.
And to devoted fathers like my husband.

Acknowledgments

Thank you to author Michele Summers
for driving out to the boonies for an into-the-wee-hours
brainstorming session for this story.

Thank you to my good friend and beta reader
Lani Bennett for allowing me to bounce ideas off you
for this story and others.

To Shannon Criss, Keyla Hernandez and the rest of the
Kimani editorial team, thank you for providing insight
and feedback that made the story stronger while also
allowing me to remain true to my vision.

Chapter 1

Nate Johnston entered the private dining room at his favorite seafood restaurant and froze, his expensive Italian loafers rooted to the floor.

The ghost of relationships past.

Kendra didn't need to turn around for him to recognize the woman he'd once shared his bed with; the mother of his six-year-old son. He sensed her presence—like something warm wiggling beneath his skin—the instant he stepped into the room.

Nate was in the midst of the biggest crisis of his eight-year-long professional football career. Why would his brother invite him to dinner with the woman who shattered his heart seven years ago?

"Glad you're here, Nate. Have a seat." His brother Marcus indicated the seat next to Kendra.

Nate narrowed his gaze at his brother and took the

seat beside him instead. "You asked me to meet you for dinner to discuss the *situation*."

As if Kendra and every other sports network viewer hadn't seen the grainy cell phone footage of him in a club, after a few drinks, ripping his teammates to shreds following the ass-whipping they'd endured at the hands of their division rivals. A devastating loss that put the brakes on the Memphis Marauders play-off run for the third year in a row.

The video had been edited to make him look like the villain. It didn't include him detailing how his own mistakes—a dropped pass and a costly fumble—had contributed to the loss.

"That's why she's here." Marcus's response was terse. As Nate's sports agent, Marcus's job had become ten times harder since the tape hit the airwaves that morning.

"Hello, Nate." Kendra's apologetic smile indicated she knew something he didn't.

Nate's attention was drawn to her expressive face. How did she manage to get more beautiful every time he saw her?

Head full of short, dark curls. Sheen on high blast. Style on point. Body-hugging knit dress in his favorite color on her—Marauders blue. The color perfectly contrasted the expanse of smooth brown skin exposed by the neckline of her dress.

An uneasy feeling crawled up his spine. Nate turned to his brother. "What do you mean *that's why she's here*?"

"It means we've got a ton of damage control to do, in addition to negotiating your new contract with the Marauders and trying to renew your two biggest endorsement deals. I can't handle everything alone. I've asked for Kendra's assistance."

Marcus had every right to be pissed, and Nate expected a little brotherly payback. But Marcus was a few cans short of a six-pack if he expected him to work with the woman who left him on one knee, ring in hand.

"What's wrong with the PR firm we've been using?"

"They're great when things are good, but we're in crisis mode. We need someone tough who'll get ahead of this thing and change the narrative out there about you."

"And out of all the possibilities in the free world, you believe the woman who rejected my proposal is the best person for the job?" He slid his gaze to Kendra. Her cheeks glowed beneath her warm, dark skin.

A twinge of guilt settled in his gut. It was a low blow, but so was walking out on him when he asked her to marry him seven years ago. He'd convinced himself he was over it and her. Yet the rejection still stung, especially being relegated to a part-time father.

Nate's father had tucked him and his six siblings into bed every night. Read them stories, taught them how to fish, fix their bikes and change the brakes on a car. He was still very much part of their lives. Nate had looked forward to being the kind of father who was present in his kids' lives every day.

Kendra had destroyed his chance of being that kind of dad to Kai.

When she'd responded to his marriage proposal by walking out, she'd left a hole in his chest where his heart had once been. Discovering the pregnancy a few weeks later, then announcing she fully intended to raise the baby on her own, had ripped out his soul and left him in a tailspin.

He still couldn't forgive her for reducing him to a baby daddy. For being the reason he didn't get to tuck Kai into bed most nights. Now Marcus wanted to put his future in her hands?

Oh, hell naw.

"I *know* she's the best person for the job." Marcus's expression was unwavering.

"I understand why you're still upset." Kendra's eyes conveyed the apology he'd already heard too many times. "But this isn't about our past. It's about ensuring your future on your terms. I can help you do that because I'm damn good at what I do. But I don't want to be here if you don't want me here."

"Good, then it's settled. What's for dinner?" Nate picked up his menu.

Marcus pushed the menu down. "Don't be a smartass, Nate. More importantly, don't let your ego get in the way of what's best for your career and your bank account. You've dug a king-size hole for yourself, little brother. It's my job to get you back on solid ground. I can do that, but I need Dray's help."

Nate narrowed his gaze at Marcus. *Dray? Really?* They were suddenly cozy enough that his brother was using the nickname he'd called her when they were together?

He turned his attention to Kendra. Her arms were folded, inadvertently pressing her breasts higher. His heartbeat quickened and his throat suddenly felt dry.

Focus, buddy, and not on those.

He gulped water from his glass, then cleared his throat. "I don't doubt your ability, Kendra, but given our history, working together is ill-advised. Am I the only one who gets that?"

"It's an awkward situation," Kendra acknowledged with a soft sigh, "but you're Kai's father. We'll always have a connection. Whether you believe it or not, Nate, I want what's best for you. That hasn't changed."

Nate swallowed the lump in his throat. "Let's not pretend this *is* a charitable arrangement. It's your chance to make a name for yourself."

Kendra pursed her lips painted a rich, velvety red reminiscent of a full-bodied glass of vintage port. As proud and stubborn as her mother, the woman was allergic to accepting help. It had taken him nearly a year to convince her to accept child support for Kai.

"This *is* an opportunity for me, which means I'm invested in your success. When we worked together, informally, you were a media darling."

Nate tapped his finger on the table. Kendra wasn't wrong. She'd been a huge help back then. He'd even asked her to help a couple of his college buddies who'd run into trouble.

He sucked in a deep breath. "You're good, but that isn't the point."

"Then what is the point?" She leaned forward, her arms folded, elbows on the table, providing an excellent view of her cleavage.

Nate was beginning to think she was doing it on purpose. Distracting him and trying to get him off his game. He swallowed hard, ignoring the blood emptying from his brain and rushing below his belt.

He glanced over at his smirking brother, who seemed to enjoy watching Kendra take him to task.

"You're going to make me say it? Fine." Nate leaned

forward, palms pressed to the table. "I prefer to work with someone I know has my back. Someone who'll ride this out instead of hitting the door the second the road gets hard. I want to work with someone who'll stand their ground and fight for me."

Kendra grimaced, as if he'd knocked the wind out of her.

Part of him relished the pain evident in her eyes. It didn't begin to rival the pain she'd inflicted on him. Yet another part of him couldn't bear to see the hurt in her chocolate-brown eyes.

"Your feelings are valid." Marcus spoke after what felt like a full minute of silence. His tone was apologetic, though Nate wasn't sure if the apology was meant for him or Kendra. "That's why you two need to hash things out."

"You're not hearing me, Marcus. There is nothing for us to hash out."

Marcus placed a firm hand on his shoulder. "You're my brother. I'd take a bullet for you. But as your agent, I have to be the voice of reason. Tell you what you need to hear. You screwed up. Royally. At the worst possible time. This is mission-critical. We need Dray. She knows you better than anyone, and she's a master at crisis management. Besides, she has a vested interest in seeing you succeed. All of our futures are on the line here, Nate. I wouldn't bring Dray in if I didn't trust her implicitly."

Kendra gave Marcus a grateful smile. She sat taller and returned her attention to Nate. "I can do this, Nate. I won't let you down."

Nate ignored her plea. He turned to Marcus. "I think we're pushing the panic button here."

"Cards on the table, bro?" Marcus motioned for the server to come over. "It was Bat-Signal time the second that video hit the airwaves. The building is on fire. Don't be too proud to accept the help of a friendly face wearing a cape and toting a fire hose."

Nate gritted his teeth as Kendra held back a grin, her eyes gleaming. He sat stewing as Marcus explained to the server that he'd be leaving, so she should deliver his meal and the bill to Nate.

He loved his family, but it was a universal truth that older brothers could be asses.

Marcus stood and slipped on his wool coat. He gripped Nate's shoulder. "You said you'd do whatever it took to make this right. I'm playing that card now. You're two adults with a common goal. Figure it out." He shifted his gaze to Kendra. "Walk me out?"

She grabbed her wrap and followed him out.

Damn.

Next time he'd be careful with the promises he made his brother. His only hope was to convince Kendra to walk away.

Again.

Chapter 2

"You seem pleased." Kendra pulled the wrap tightly around her shoulders to combat the biting winter wind rushing into the lobby as patrons entered and exited. It was an unusual cold spell for North Carolina. "I'm not sure we were in the same room, because Nate isn't buying this."

"Not yet, but then you were prepared to turn me down when you arrived. What changed your mind?"

Her cheeks warmed. She agreed to dinner because she'd been intrigued by Marcus's proposal. It was her chance to finally establish a boutique PR and media coaching firm that catered to high-end talent. But she'd decided to take Nate on as a client the moment she laid eyes on him. Six feet three inches of brown-skin Adonis. Handsome and fit as ever. There was no way she'd admit that to his brother or to anyone.

"Despite what Nate thinks, he needs my help. Besides, I owe him." She couldn't erase the pain she'd caused when she'd walked away seven years ago, but she could make things right for him. Allow him to end his career on his terms.

Marcus squeezed her arm. "You don't owe either of us anything, but I'm glad you're on board."

"This isn't a done deal. I meant what I said. I'm willing to work through Nate resenting my help, but I won't do this if he's resistant. If he won't listen to me, this doesn't work."

"Then you've got some convincing to do." Marcus winked, tipped the valet and drove off.

Great. Kendra drew in a deep breath, then strutted back into the restaurant, spine straight and tall. *You've got this, girl.*

Nate didn't bother standing when she returned. He stared as if he couldn't believe she had the nerve to sashay her tail back into the private dining room. As if he'd expected her to turn and run.

"You need convincing, so let's talk. Ask me anything you want. We can discuss the ideas I have so far or the crisis management work I've done for high-profile corporate clients."

The server set their meals on the table. When she left, Nate took a swig of his beer, then set the glass on the table with a *thud*. "Fine. Let's talk about what happened between us."

"Nate…" Her voice wavered for a moment. She cleared her throat and lengthened her spine, holding his gaze. "We've talked about this."

"'I'm so sorry, Nate, I just can't do this' isn't a discussion, Kendra." The veins in his neck corded as he repeated her words that night verbatim. "You've shut me down anytime I've tried to have a real conversation about that night. If you want me to trust you, start by being honest about what happened between us."

"This isn't productive." She shivered beneath his cold stare. "Discussing my proposed PR plan is."

"If Marcus says you can do the job, I trust his judgment. What I need is to know I can trust you. So for once, be honest with me about why you walked out. Why you waited until I asked you to marry me and you were pregnant with my son to decide I wasn't the right man for you."

Her heart clenched at the bitterness that laced his words. It took her back to that night. The night she'd made the biggest mistake of her life.

"I underestimated how difficult it was to be the wife of a pro athlete."

"I'd been with the Marauders for a year by then. How would your life have been any different?"

"There's a huge difference between being the live-in girlfriend and being the wife and mother of your children."

"A marriage license is just a piece of paper, Kendra. Other than having it and my last name, nothing would've changed."

She tipped her chin, determined to keep her emotions in check. "It isn't a meaningless piece of paper. It's a lifelong commitment. That means something to me."

Nate snorted. "If it means so much to you, why'd you turn it down when I offered it?"

"I couldn't be one of those football wives who

doesn't have a life of her own and pretends not to know what happens on the road."

His expression morphed from anger to hurt again. "So it was about that girl who let herself into my room in Cleveland. I told you, I didn't know her, and nothing happened between us. When I discovered her in my room, I called security and they sent her ass packing. End of story. I called you right away and told you about it. I wasn't trying to hide anything."

"The sports channels picked up the story. I would've heard about it."

Nate ran a hand through his close-cropped curls and heaved a sigh. "So that's what you think of me? That the minute I'm out of sight I can't keep it in my pants? News flash, Kendra, if I'd wanted to be with someone else, I would've been. Football groupies have been throwing themselves at me since high school. I didn't want them. I wanted you. I loved you. You obviously didn't feel the same."

"That isn't true." The accusation hit her like a bullet to the chest, piercing her heart and severing arteries. Nate was the only man she'd ever loved. She loved him still, but their time was past, and it was all her fault. "I'm a realist. You're only human. A man can only take so much temptation."

"If you felt that way, you should've come to me. We could've worked things out."

"How, Nate? You weren't going to leave the team, and I'd never ask *you* to give up your dream." She hadn't meant to stress the word.

Nate shifted in his seat, lowering his gaze. He hadn't missed the implication. She'd supported his dream, but he hadn't supported hers. He took another sip of his beer. "I never gave you any reason to doubt me."

"It was my issue, not yours. I fully own that."

"Just to be clear, you blew up our relationship, our family, because you thought I *might* eventually cheat on you?"

"It isn't as simple as that." She poked at the flounder she no longer had an appetite for. "My fears are very real, and I have them for good reason. That's my problem, not yours."

Nate laughed bitterly. "It sure as hell felt like my problem when you turned down my proposal in a roomful of our family and friends."

She cringed, remembering the moment he dropped to one knee and presented her with a beautiful, custom diamond engagement ring. The memory of that moment was as vivid now as it was then. Euphoric joy immediately followed by debilitating fear and a panic attack that stole her breath.

Chest heaving and the room spinning, she had only one clear thought—she couldn't marry Nate.

Until that moment, she'd anticipated the day he'd propose and dreamed of an intimate wedding ceremony on the beach. Then Nate asked her to marry him and the room went black.

Visions of ruthless groupies who'd do anything to get with a ballplayer filled her head. Her own father hadn't been faithful to her mother. How could she expect Nate to do so with so much temptation?

She'd broken it off, packed her things and made the long drive back to Pleasure Cove. Weeks later, she discovered she was pregnant with Kai.

"You didn't deserve that. I should've told you how I'd been feeling, but—"

"You didn't trust me enough to have an honest discussion then. Give me one reason I should trust you now." The ache reflected in his dark eyes penetrated her skin more than the bone-chilling air outside had.

Kendra choked back the thickness in her throat. "Because I'm the same girl who cheered you on at every game from peewee to the pros. The one who wouldn't let you give up on your dream when you weren't drafted."

Nate's expression softened, but he didn't respond.

Encouraged, Kendra continued. "We were so young then, Nate. I handled my feelings poorly. But I've never been anything but supportive of your career, and I've proven that I'm willing to go to bat for you. Who was it that convinced those arena football teams to give you a shot? Who sent your arena highlight clips to pro teams until the Marauders invited you to try out?"

"You." He rubbed his chin. "I owe my entire career to you."

"Our relationship may have ended, but my support of your career hasn't. No consultant will fight for your career harder than I will. Deep down, I think you know that."

Nate kneaded the back of his neck. "Okay, fine."

"Really?"

"Just until we secure my new contract."

Her buzz was quickly doused—like a too-short candlewick. The muscles of her face strained to maintain her smile. "Of course."

"We'll make it a six-month contract. You'll be well

paid and Marcus will give you references, contacts…
anything you need to rebrand your business. All right?"

"It's a generous offer, thank you. I accept."

"All right then." Nate inhaled Kendra's sweet scent:
a gentle breeze wafting through a summer garden
bursting with jasmine and gardenias. He pretended
not to notice the disappointment on her face. It tugged
at his heart and made him want to promise her the
world just to see a genuine smile light those brown
eyes. "I'll call Marcus tonight and have him draw up
the contract."

"Great, I'll have my lawyer review it and we can
go from there."

"How is your brother doing?" Nate sipped his
beer, amused by how formally Kendra referred to her
brother, Dashon, a contract law attorney.

Kendra shrugged. "He's still Dash. Being himself
and doing his own thing."

"New York must be treating him well. I hear he
rarely returns to Pleasure Cove." Nate carved into his
prime rib covered with a creamy mushroom and lobster sauce—one of Nadine's specialties.

Kendra's mouth twisted. He'd obviously touched a
nerve. He wouldn't pry further. They didn't need to
be best friends. Just have a personable working relationship. "He comes home about as often as Quincy."

Touché. His globe-trotting younger brother was
quickly making a name for himself as a photographer. His shadow rarely darkened the Johnston family's doorstep.

Nate contemplated the quiet look of concern that

furrowed Kendra's brows. "Did I say something wrong?"

She stopped pushing the food around her plate and put down her fork. "No, but there's something we need to address, so I'm just going to say it."

He put down his utensils and sat back warily. "I'm listening."

"What happened between us in Memphis—"

"Which time?" Nate couldn't help the smirk that tightened his mouth when he remembered how an argument between them had descended into hot, angry sex on two different occasions.

"Both." Kendra clearly wasn't amused. Nor did she seem to have the same fond memories of those occasions. "That can't happen again."

"I was hoping it would be one of the amenities you'd throw into the deal." He held back a grin as he drained the last of his beer.

She pointed one of her painted fingernails at him. "See, that's what I'm talking about. If this is going to work, you have to take me seriously."

"Oh, I took what we did very seriously." He raised an eyebrow and resumed eating his meal.

She let out a frustrated sigh and settled back in her seat. "This is your career we're talking about here, Nate. I need to maintain my focus, and I can't stay focused on cleaning up your rep if I'm thinking about…" Her words trailed off and there was a deep flush in her cheeks beneath her smooth brown skin. She shook her head, as if trying to shake off the memories. "Neither of us can afford the distraction."

"Agreed." He adjusted in his chair, his own body reacting to the memories. Her scent. Her taste. The sound of her soft pleas. "Though it worries me that my media consultant can't multitask."

They dissolved into laughter, and for a moment, it felt like old times. It was the first time either of them seemed relaxed since he'd arrived.

Nate smiled, relishing the sound of her laughter. One of the countless details about her he missed. "Okay, Ms. Media Consultant, where do we begin?"

Chapter 3

"This sounds like a great opportunity." Maya Alvarez, Kendra's half sister, sipped her mocha latte as they sat at the breakfast bar in the gorgeous penthouse Maya shared with her fiancé, hotelier Liam Westbrook. "So why aren't you excited about it?"

Kendra took a sip of the frothy peppermint mocha her sister made for her and let out an appreciative moan. "I am, but what if I'm jumping out of the frying pan and into the fire?"

"It's a tricky situation. I certainly couldn't work with the girls' dad. Not for all the money in the world." Maya placed a hand on Kendra's in response to her fallen expression. "But it's different with you and Nate."

"How? Carlos walked out on you, just like I walked out on Nate. The only difference was you and Carlos were married." Kendra drank more of her coffee. "He feels the same way you do. Honestly, I can't blame him."

"You've maintained an amicable relationship. Friendly enough that you two hooked up." Maya peered over her coffee cup, her dark eyes dancing with amusement.

"Shut. Up." Kendra pointed a finger at her giggling sister. "I shouldn't have told you that. I still can't believe it happened. Twice."

"Are we talking instances or the actual amount of times you guys—"

"Stop it, Maya!" Kendra's face and neck warmed. "Everyone knows you're not supposed to hold the things your sister says when she's drunk against her."

"All right, fine." Maya was still giggling. "I'm just saying, things can't be *that* bad between you. Besides, Nate's a terrific guy, and we both know you still have feelings for him."

"Of course I care about him. That doesn't mean we should be together." It was too quiet without the children around. Nothing to distract her from a conversation she'd rather not have. Liam had taken them to see the aquariums he'd just had installed at his family's luxury resort so she and Maya could talk. "Things between us are…complicated."

"Things were complicated for us, too. Every day I'm grateful Liam recognized that what we have was worth fighting for, despite the complications." Maya's face glowed when she spoke of Liam.

Kendra missed that feeling—the infinite joy of being in love with a man who adored her. She ignored the growing sense of envy that felt like a boulder tethered to her ankle, threatening to drown her in a sea of self-pity. She forced a smile. "I'm happy for you. You're perfect together, and Liam is so good with the kids."

"Sofie and Ella adore him."

"So does Kai. He talks about his Uncle Liam all the time. You'd think he was a superhero or something. He's making the Johnston men jealous."

"Liam has really taken to Kai, too." A warm smile lit Maya's eyes like a candle lighting a paper lantern from within.

No matter how many times Kendra saw that smile— and it was often in the weeks since Liam and Maya had gotten engaged—she couldn't stop her reaction to it. Intense joy for her sister, followed by deep sorrow for herself.

Maya seemed to recognize her pain. Her brows furrowed with concern. "I'm glad you accepted the offer, but I'm a little worried, too. Are you sure you're going to be okay with this? Six months is a long time."

"This is my shot to finally build the kind of clientele I've always wanted. I'm not going to blow it. Besides, Nate needs my help. I know it won't make up for how I hurt him, but at least it's something."

"When is your first meeting?"

"Tomorrow, so I'd better get it together."

Maya's smile was reassuring. "Everything will be fine, and who knows? Maybe you two will make up."

"Don't even go there, and please don't give Kai false hope about me and his dad getting back together. I don't think he could bear that. He misses him so much when he's away during the season. Now that the girls have Liam in their lives, Kai is more aware of his father's absence."

"I didn't realize—"

Kendra squeezed her sister's forearm. "I'm thankful Liam's in his life. What he's feeling now…it would've come up eventually. We'll deal with it. He'll be fine."

"Either way, I know this is going to work out for the best. You have to believe that."

"It has to. If Nate ends up with a West Coast team, Kai will see him even less. He'd be heartbroken." Kendra's voice wavered. She sipped her coffee, hoping her sister didn't notice. "If I can prevent that from happening, I have to at least try."

Kendra avoided Maya's gaze and the pity she knew she'd see there. They both turned toward the front door in response to the jangling of keys that signaled Liam and the children's arrival.

Kai practically jumped into her arms. He was a sweet, affectionate boy. She kissed her son's forehead, dreading the days when he got older and would think it uncool to give her a big hug and a sloppy kiss.

She took in her handsome, smiling child. Wide, round eyes. Nate's nose—a narrow bridge with slightly flared nostrils. A wide smile stretched his Cupid's bow mouth—a near duplicate of hers. His thick ringlets were cut into a frohawk. He was only six, but his long arms and legs indicated he would be tall—like his father.

Kai was the perfect mélange of her and Nate's features, and he'd inherited an ideal mix of their personalities. He was truly the best of them.

Kendra smiled, warmth spreading through her chest as she choked back tears. Maybe she didn't get their relationship right, but she would always have the best part of Nate.

For that she was grateful.

Chapter 4

Nate fluffed the pillows on the sofa in his office for the third time, then readjusted the chain on his neck again.

This isn't a date. It's business. Be cool.

He eased onto the sofa and drummed his fingers on his knee. Kendra would arrive shortly for their first official meeting.

She and Marcus had met before the ink dried so she could lay out her ideas and they could come to consensus on a plan. Marcus had thought it was best for him to sit out that meeting.

Fine by him.

He recognized the necessity of jumping through PR hoops. Still, he resented wasting time and money defending himself about truthful comments made in private.

Not that there was any such thing as privacy any-more in the social media age.

A car door slammed. Nate glanced at his watch and smiled. On time, as always. Kendra was right; in many ways, she hadn't changed. Organized and efficient, she'd never been late for anything.

Nate opened the door before Kendra could ring the bell, startling her. She dropped her leather portfolio, her papers sailing across the porch.

He planned to help her recover them, but froze, mesmerized by the perfectly round shape of her curvy bottom in a narrow black pencil skirt as she bent to re-trieve them. Finally shaken from his daze, he stooped to pick up a few sheets that had landed near his feet. He handed them to her, his fingertips grazing her soft skin.

Kendra withdrew her hand, as if she, too, felt the spark of electricity that charged his skin when they touched. She gave him an uneasy smile as she accepted the papers and stuffed them back into the portfolio. "Not the graceful entrance I hoped to make."

"Also not quite as entertaining as your entrance to the junior prom." He grinned.

"You did not just go there. You're never going to forget that, are you?"

He chuckled. "Don't think anyone in Pleasure Cove ever will. Principal Dansby nearly crapped himself when you came strolling up to the stage in your pur-ple Prince tribute gown with your right butt cheek on display."

Kendra shuddered, shifting the portfolio to her other arm. Her cheeks glowed red beneath her dark brown skin. "You know the ass-baring feature was completely unintentional. I told my mother wearing panty hose was a bad idea. If I hadn't been wearing them, my dress couldn't have gotten tucked into the back of them. I still blame her for the entire fiasco."

"We managed to have a good time, despite getting tossed out—thanks to your indecent exposure." He smiled at the warm memory of the two of them strolling on the beach that night, hand in hand.

They'd crashed a sunset wedding on the beach. Kendra had been moved by the ceremony, her eyes brimming with tears. She said it was the most perfect thing she'd ever seen. He wiped the tears from her face and promised to marry her one day in a sunset ceremony right there on that beach.

He'd attempted to keep his promise, but look how that turned out. Nate shook his head, purging the memory from his brain. Jaw stiff, his hands clenched into fists.

Kendra seemed aware of the shift in his mood. She clutched her portfolio. "Is this still a good time?"

"As good as any." He opened the door wider and stepped aside to allow her to enter.

"This place looks incredible." Her eyes danced as she glanced around the open space. "I haven't been here since they first broke ground."

That had been by design. He'd bought the land and had this place constructed because he expected to build a life here with her. To one day watch their children surf the same beaches they'd surfed together as kids. When everything fell apart, he'd done his damnedest to keep her out of the space that was meant to be theirs.

"Thanks." He crammed his hands into the pockets of his jeans. "Can I take your coat or get you anything before we get started?"

She removed her wrap, unveiling a low-cut silk blouse that complemented her curves nicely. "That coffee smells great. I'd love a cup."

"Coming up." He headed for the kitchen. "Is it okay if we work in here today?"

"Of course. I want to make this as convenient as possible. I'm willing to accommodate your schedule in any way necessary." Kendra set her portfolio and laptop on the black, poured concrete kitchen countertop.

He grabbed two mugs from the cabinet, filled her cup, added cream and handed it to her.

Kendra thanked him and settled onto her seat, then opened her laptop and pulled two copies of a thick, bound document from her leather bag. She handed him one and opened the other. "I'd like to give you the overview of the plan Marcus and I agreed on."

Nate thumbed through the document quickly. Neat, efficient, color-coded. *Very Kendra.* He dropped it onto the countertop with a *thud.* Leaning back in his seat, he sipped his coffee. "Shoot."

Nate was determined to make her turn and run, just as she had seven years ago. Well, they were beyond that. She'd signed her name to a contract and walked away from her most lucrative client.

No turning back.

She'd stayed up late the past few nights working on the proposal, and Nate wouldn't give it more than a cursory glance?

Fine.

She hadn't expected him to give in easily. But if he was already annoyed with her treatise on how to get his career back on track, he certainly wasn't going to like the steps she'd outlined.

Too bad.

This was what needed to happen if he wanted to get out of this predicament and land his new contract and endorsements.

Kendra met his defiant gaze. "Our campaign will focus on three strategies. First, you need to meet with each person you mentioned on that tape and apologize. Talk to them man-to-man and explain what happened—before we go public. Call anyone you can't get a sit-down with. Then we make the public apology."

Nate was growing more agitated by the minute. He folded his arms. "If I'm apologizing to each of them individually, what's the purpose of a public apology?"

"You said your tight end was more concerned with his individual stats than winning a championship. That your quarterback, and long-time friend, has been dialing it in all year. You slammed your defensive players for skating on their natural talents and having poor work ethics. And you claimed your running back is three years past his expiration date. All of that is public. So your apology needs to be, too."

"It's not like I didn't call myself out for my mistakes, too. Funny how they didn't include that part."

"I get it. That makes me believe that this Stephanie Weiss who broke the story is out to get you. This was calculated. Vindictive."

Nate bristled at the mention of Stephanie's name. "If they were going to leak the video, I just wish they'd shown everything."

"Fortunately, someone leaked the full video. Probably the person who actually recorded it. At the press conference, we'll play the missing part where you skewer your own mistakes, too. Then you'll make a statement. We'll go from the emotional angle of the disappointment you were feeling—with yourself and the rest of the team. Any sports fan can sympathize with that. Explain that while the critique was your honest assessment of what led to the loss, you regret the harsh words you used to express it."

Nate's lips puckered like he was sucking on a lemon. He nearly drained his coffee mug. "Fine. Anything else?"

"Be honest. Tell them your team is your family, and like most family disputes, this one will be resolved behind closed doors, not in the public arena."

"Won't they want to ask questions?"

"Doesn't mean you have to answer them." She shrugged. "We'll establish from the outset that you won't be entertaining questions."

"That's an idea I can get behind," he mumbled. "What's the second strategy?"

"We have to change the narrative out there about you on our terms. We'll cherry-pick media outlets that are trustworthy, but we'll lay the ground rules about which topics are off-limits."

"If I'm not talking about the tape—which is what they're all going to want to talk about—what am I there to discuss?"

"At this time of year, there are a million opportunities to discuss the play-off games—on radio, television, newspapers and blogs. You can offer your razor-sharp game analysis there. Plus, you'll set yourself up for a career as an analyst once you retire."

Nate shrugged. "I could do that, I guess."

"And you'll be phenomenal at it." Kendra smiled, encouraged that Nate had taken well to at least part of the plan. "You'll also need to talk about your philanthropy."

He frowned, his eyebrows forming angry slashes over his dark eyes. "The Johnston Family Foundation isn't some cheap publicity stunt. I'm not looking to blow my own horn."

"I know, which makes the work you do all the more admirable." She held up a hand, holding off the next wave of protest. "But just think how much more good you could do if you publicized the work you're doing with wounded veterans and high-risk children from low-income families."

Nate stood and paced the floor. "Our clients have been through enough. They need someone to give them a hand, not someone else who only sees them as a means to their own end. No." He shook his head. "I won't do it."

Kendra inhaled deeply, then took a different approach. One Nate might better understand.

"You don't want to take advantage of your clients. I admire that. But if we can't repair your reputation, you won't be in a position to help them as much as you'd like."

He didn't respond, but stopped pacing and rested his chin on his closed fist.

"Besides, if more companies—including your current sponsors—were aware of the programs your foundation offers and the difference you're making in people's lives, they'd want to contribute. That means you'll be able to help even more people. Isn't that what you want?"

"You know I do, but I won't betray their trust."

"I'd never ask you to do that." Kendra softened her voice. "All I'm asking is that you give them the opportunity to help themselves and others. I'm sure a lot of the families your foundation has helped would be eager to participate in a goodwill campaign to spread the word and increase funding."

Nate dropped into his seat, as if he were exhausted from a fight. "Fine. I'll agree to *some* media coverage for the foundation programs, but I need final approval on anything we put out there."

"Absolutely." She hoped he didn't see how relieved she was. "Any other concerns?"

"Yeah. What if the interviewers aren't willing to stick to the script?"

She nodded solemnly. "Always a possibility. One we'll make sure you're prepared to handle in a way that won't aggravate the situation."

"You make it sound so easy."

"It will be." She smiled, hoping to reassure him.

"And the third strategy? Do I even want to know what it is?"

He knew her well enough to know she'd saved the option he'd like least for last.

"It's time for you to come out of the Stone Age and start using social media."

"C'mon, Kendra. I've got a crisis on my hands. You said so yourself. I don't have time to mess around on social media."

"The public is only seeing you through the filter of the news media and talking heads out there. Social media puts you in control of your own message, in real time. Your fans—and potential sponsors—will get a better sense of who you are."

He shook his head slowly, thoughtfully. A marked improvement over the adamant refusal issued moments earlier. "The last thing I want is more people in my business."

"I understand your reluctance. Especially in light of what's happened. The reality is, they're already in your business. This way you become the gatekeeper. You let them in, but in a way you completely control."

Nate grunted. "Don't really have a choice, do I?"

Kendra tried to hold back her grin. "Not really, but I promise to make it as painless as possible. I'll actually be running the accounts for you, so it won't be as much work as you're imagining. Promise."

He nodded reluctantly. "If you really think this is the only way we win, okay. I'll do it. Anything else we need to discuss?" His posture was tense. As if he couldn't wait to get her out of his house.

She tried to pretend it didn't hurt that he wanted her as far away from him as possible. "Actually, there is something else we need to discuss. What's the story on Stephanie Weiss?"

Nate frowned. "Marcus didn't tell you?"

"He thought it would be better if you explained." She shifted in her chair. "I gather you two were together at some point, or Marcus wouldn't have been so cryptic about your connection."

"Not one of my best decisions." He tapped a finger on the countertop, staring beyond her. "Stephanie dragged me into the middle of a scandal back then that nearly ruined my relationship with my teammates. Now she's done it again."

"Exactly what happened with her?" She sighed when he narrowed his gaze at her. "If I'm going to help you, I need to understand what's going on, and not just what I've read on the internet. I need the complete picture. We can't afford to get blindsided again."

An uncomfortable silence settled over them as he stared out the window onto the backyard. He didn't want to talk to one ex about another.

She got that. She'd probably feel the same. Still, she needed to know more about this Stephanie Weiss. Beyond what she learned from watching her reports online and reading her bio. And if she was being honest, it wasn't just her professional curiosity that needed to be satisfied. "Did you love her?"

He scowled, the corners of his mouth pinched. His resentment of the question rolled off him in waves. His answer was quiet, but emphatic. "No."

Kendra went to the coffee machine and refilled her cup. She held her hand out for his. "You don't have to worry about hurting my feelings. I'm a big girl. I can handle the truth."

"I told you the truth. I wasn't in love with her." He thrust his empty cup into her hand. "We were only together a few months. What difference does it make, anyway?"

"Helps me understand her frame of mind. If we're dealing with a woman scorned nursing a vendetta, we need to stay two steps ahead of her." She returned the mug to him, filled with black coffee.

"That's the only reason you want to know?" He peered at her over the rim of his mug as he took a sip of his coffee.

She returned to her seat and tapped a few keys on her computer, waking the screen up. "Of course."

He smirked, unconvinced. With good reason. She was lying through her teeth.

"So, what led to this scandal and why does she have it in for you?" Kendra put down her mug, prepared to type her notes.

"Do we really need to get into all of this? It's ancient history."

"Not to her, I'm guessing."

"Stephanie was listening to my phone calls. Checking my text messages. She discovered a teammate of mine was in serious trouble. She broke the story using the info she'd gathered, saying it was from an unnamed source. When I read the story, I recognized what she'd done. Since we were dating, my teammates and the public believed I'd been feeding Stephanie information. I broke it off with her, publicly denied I was the source and discredited her story." He frowned. "She was fired, and none of the top media outlets wanted anything to do with her."

"I'm sorry you ended up in the middle of it."

"Should've known better than to sleep with the enemy, right?"

"Real journalists aren't your enemy. They won't always give you the glowing praise you want, but the good ones are honest and fair. They're only interested in the truth. Those are the media personalities we need to make our allies."

"Good luck finding any of those." He finished his coffee and moved to the sink to rinse his cup.

"Got a few in mind. I think you'll be pleased."

He grunted, his biceps bulging as he folded his arms

over his chest. The gray quick-dry athletic material stretched to accommodate his firm pecs. He flipped his wrist and checked his watch. "Anything else?"

Kendra swallowed, her throat suddenly dry. Nate seemed fully aware of her reaction to him and utterly pleased with himself for evoking it. She shook her head. "No, I think we're good. For now. I'll keep you updated. Marcus's assistant, Kara, gave me access to your calendar. I'll add any interviews and appearances as I book them."

"All right." He pinned her with his gaze. "Is that all?"

"Kara will make the flight arrangements for your apology tour once you request meetings with each of the guys. I'd begin with Marauders' owner Bud Flynn and then the head coach."

The smug expression crumbled. "Why? I didn't say anything about either of them."

"This media circus is disruptive to the entire team. Besides, Bud has been like a second father to you. He gave you your big break. Don't you think you owe him an apology?"

Nate sighed. "I'll call him as soon as I'm done."

"Good."

"Don't mean to rush you." He checked his watch again. "But I have another appointment."

"Right. Sorry. I know you're busy." Kendra put on her wrap and packed up her things. She slipped her bag on her shoulder, tucked the portfolio under her arm and turned around, nearly running into Nate.

"Look, I know I'm not the easiest guy to work with, but I do appreciate the work you've put into this." He leaned in closer, his warm breath whispering against her skin. "And I just want you to know..."

The doorbell rang. Nate sighed and cursed under his breath before turning toward the door.

"Nate, what were you going to say?" Kendra followed him, her heart beating hard. Something in her desperately needed to know what Nate was going to say before they'd been interrupted by the bell.

"Doesn't matter." He shook his head then turned to open the door.

"I came a few minutes early so we could work on those positions you had so much trouble with the other day." A tall, gorgeous blonde wearing a short skirt, a cropped top and thigh-high boots floated inside carrying a large duffel that looked like it weighed twice as much as she did. The woman finally noticed Kendra. "Oh, I'm sorry, I didn't realize you had company."

"I was just leaving." Kendra forced a polite smile.

Nate placed his hand low on the woman's back and introduced them. "Layne, this is Kendra—Kai's mom. She'll be handling my PR. Kendra, this is my friend Layne."

Layne gave Nate an odd smile before offering Kendra a limp handshake. "Pleased to meet you. I've heard so much about you." She turned to Nate without waiting for a response. "I'll go ahead and get everything set up."

"Great. Thanks, Layne."

The woman sauntered off, obviously familiar with the house.

"She's pretty." The words came out before Kendra could reel them back in. "She's built like a dancer."

Nate smirked, holding the door open a bit wider. "She takes great care of her body. And mine."

"I certainly don't want to get in the way of that." Kendra forced a smile despite the deep ache in her chest at the thought of Nate and Ms. Ballerina Body doing God knows what. "I'll follow up tomorrow to see how the phone calls went, and if I need to run interference with anyone."

"Don't think that'll be necessary, but thank you. Kiss li'l man for me. Tell him Dad's got a surprise for him this weekend."

Before she could respond, he'd closed the door behind her. The sound echoed in her head like the closing of a vault.

Maybe she was still nursing feelings for Nate, but he'd obviously gotten over her.

Chapter 5

Nate sank into the whirlpool after his hot yoga session with Layne and made his calls.

He'd tucked his tail and done a good bit of explaining. First to Bud Flynn, then to Coach Emerson. Bud was out of the country. He tentatively accepted Nate's apology by phone, but insisted they meet in person once he returned. He scheduled a meeting with Coach Emerson.

Nate left a message for two of his teammates and had incredibly awkward conversations with a few others.

Except for the team's quarterback, Wade Willis, who agreed his performance had been subpar, none of the guys went easy on him. Eating a king-size slice of humble pie was exactly what he deserved for running his big mouth.

Tomorrow he'd board a plane to meet with Wade

at his ranch in Montana. Then he'd head to Memphis for meetings with Coach Emerson and Lee Davis, the head of team personnel. He dreaded the meeting with Lee—the only member of the Marauders' front office he'd never really seen eye-to-eye with. Lee had been itching to trade him, and the video scandal was just the ammunition he needed.

Nate slipped deeper into the water, allowing the warmth to wash over his aching muscles. The heat eased the tension in his shoulders and worked out the kinks in his back.

After eight years in the league, he was nursing his fair share of injuries. Each season it became more difficult to rebound from the beating his body took on any given Sunday.

If he were smart, he'd forget about a new contract and retire. Accept that he was a great player in his own right, but would never know the pride of hoisting a championship trophy. He'd be in good company. A host of athletes in every major sport were on that list.

Still, he wasn't ready to give up. The Marauders were a few pieces shy of being a contender with a legitimate shot at the championship. He shifted to get the knot in his back closer to the jet.

His recent actions certainly hadn't made the task of getting the Marauders championship-ready any easier.

Closing his eyes, he tried to relax—something he'd never been very good at. His brain seemed to go a mile a minute—even when he slept.

Nate massaged the knot that formed in his neck as he recalled the hurt and anger in each man's voice. The tension he'd created between them. Then there was the meeting with Kendra.

His body reacted to the vivid vision of her that crept over his senses. Kendra was sexy as ever in that fitted skirt and a low-cut blouse. He'd had to shove his hands in his pockets, not trusting that he'd keep his hands to himself.

When she spoke, he'd been mesmerized by her lips, overwhelmed with the desire to taste her mouth and slide his fingers in her dark curls.

Get it together, man.

He shook his head and stood, the chilly air assaulting his wet skin. Nate stepped out of the tub and slipped on a thick terry cloth robe. He slid on his sport sandals and went inside.

Nate uncapped a beer from the fridge and took a long pull. Kendra's words echoed in his head.

Neither of us can afford the distraction.

There was too much at stake. His career, the foundation and most of all…his heart. If he let her in, she'd shatter it again.

Twice, he thought he could have her body without getting caught up in the feelings they once shared.

He'd been wrong.

Kendra had walked away unscathed, while he was left brooding like a wounded animal, lashing out at everyone around him.

Nate finished his beer and tossed the bottle in the recycle bin before hopping into the shower.

This time he'd keep his hands and his heart to himself.

Kendra settled in behind the rickety old secondhand desk in her office, which doubled as the spare bedroom.

Marcus had already arranged for Nate to be a guest

on a few of the smaller sports commentary shows on the major sports network.

She reviewed the list of media personalities she'd compiled. Kendra was confident that half of the people on the list would agree to their stipulations about topics Nate wouldn't discuss. The other half were iffy, but the riskiest options offered the biggest return. She needed to see what Marcus thought of those. She dialed his cell.

Marcus answered immediately. "I was just about to ask Kara to call you."

"Why, what's up?" Kendra stopped scrolling through the list. Something in his tone told her she wouldn't like what he was about to say.

"Nate called everyone on the list."

"Great. Will he be meeting with all of them?"

"Bud Flynn's out of town. They'll meet when he gets back, but he accepted his apology, for whatever that's worth."

"And the rest of the team?"

"Wade was cool. Everyone else was pretty pissed, as we expected. Two of the guys haven't returned his calls."

"Let me guess, Tyree Thomason and Dade Hendricks." According to Nate, his relationships with the tight end and running back were strained even before the video was leaked.

"You've got it. Nate also arranged a sit-down with Lee Davis, the team's personnel manager. The guy is definitely not a fan. He's been trying to get the team to trade Nate since the upheaval Stephanie caused three years ago, but Bud Flynn won't go for it."

"Nate needs to be smart about what he says when

he talks to these guys. It's one thing to be contrite during a phone call. It's another to keep it together in person. I hope he remembers everything we talked about."

"He won't have a choice. I'm sending you with him." Marcus said the words so fast she nearly missed his meaning.

"Wait…what? We didn't discuss me going."

"I know, and I'm sorry. I don't mean to spring this on you at the last minute, but I've been thinking about it all day. It's too risky to send Nate alone."

"Then why don't you go with him?"

"I would, but I have meetings scheduled with the networks and one of the team execs. I can't miss them."

Kendra groaned. "Fine. When is he leaving?"

"Tomorrow morning."

"Are you kidding me?"

"No, and again I'm sorry about this. I realize how inconvenient this is, and I wouldn't ask if it wasn't so critical. Will your mom or Maya be able to watch Kai for a few days? If not, my mom or Alison would be happy to."

"I'll make arrangements. Just have Kara email me everything I need to know."

"Great. Oh, and Kendra?"

"Yes?"

"Pack for a week. Just in case."

Kendra ended the call and gritted her teeth. There was an empty feeling in the pit of her stomach. She curled her fingers to her palms in response to the visceral memory of the electricity she felt when Nate's fingers brushed her skin.

Sitting across the table from Nate during their first two meetings had been tough, but she'd found strength in the knowledge that their meetings would be brief. She could retreat, lick her wounds and summon her courage before it was time to do it again. Being confined on a small plane with Nate for hours would be difficult for both of them.

Kendra drew in a deep breath and picked up the phone. First, she called her mother to make arrangements for Kai. Anna Williams didn't bother to hide how ecstatic she was that Kendra would be spending the next few days on the road alone with Nate. She gladly agreed to care for Kai.

After messaging her sister to let her know about her trip, she dragged her luggage out of the closet and packed.

Kendra closed the book she was reading to Kai. He'd been asleep for at least ten minutes. She finished reading the story anyway, needing an excuse to hold him a bit longer.

She slipped her arm from beneath Kai, tucked the covers under his chin and kissed his forehead.

Her cell phone rang. She followed the sound to the kitchen, where she'd left it.

"Hey, Maya. What's up?"

"Got your message. I wanted to check on you. You sure you'll be okay on the road with Nate for an entire week?"

Kendra collapsed onto the sofa, physically drained from preparing for the trip, mentally exhausted from wrestling with the same question. "Don't really have a choice, do I?"

"We always have a choice," Maya said. "But sometimes fate pushes us in the right direction."

"You're not going to tell me you think this is the stars aligning again—like they did for you and Liam—are you?"

"Are you going to try to tell me again that you don't still have feelings for Nate?" There was a smirk in her sister's voice.

"He's my son's father, so we'll always have some sort of—"

"Connection." Maya finished her sentence. "I know, I know. That's not what I asked. I'm asking if you're still in love with him."

"We've been through this before."

"And you've never given me a straight answer." The pitch of Maya's voice rose.

"Seems like a clear hint I don't want to talk about it." Kendra paced the floor, then rearranged photos on the mantel. "So leave it alone."

"So it's all right for you to be all up in my business, but when it's your turn, suddenly you're invoking the Fifth?"

Kendra pressed a palm to her forehead. Maya usually dropped the topic once her agitation became apparent. Suddenly her sister wasn't inclined to let the subject go.

"I'm not sure how I feel," Kendra admitted. It was unsettling to hear the words spoken aloud where she could no longer hide from them. "Being around him like this…it's definitely making me feel some kind of way."

Maya's tone softened. "I know it's probably a little overwhelming, but that doesn't mean it's a bad thing. Just be open to wherever this takes you. Nate's a good guy. He adores Kai, and I have a strong feeling he's still very much in love with you."

"Don't know about that. It was kind of hard to read with his arm draped around the skinny chick who showed up at his place as he was rushing me out the door." Kendra hated the pouty tone with which she conveyed the news.

"Is he seeing her?"

"I guess so. She seemed to know her way around his place well enough. From the size of the bag she was toting, she planned to stay awhile."

"How did he introduce her?"

"As his friend."

"Well, there you go." There was a lilt in Maya's voice again. "She's his friend until we hear otherwise."

"Like you and Liam were just 'friends' over the summer?"

Maya huffed. "You're determined to ruin this, aren't you?"

"Maya, seriously, do I need to have the same talk with you I had with my mom? This is business—not a romantic getaway. Nate doesn't want me on this trip any more than I want to be on it."

"Wouldn't be so sure about that. We'll see."

"Enough with the matchmaking," Kendra said. "I still have a ton of things to do. Oh, and my mom has a doctor's appointment on Friday, so she won't be able to pick Kai up from school. Is it okay if he goes home with Sarah and the girls until my mom can pick him up?"

Liam's housekeeper, Sarah, had taken on the expanded role of part-time nanny since Maya and the girls had moved into his penthouse.

"I'm sure it won't be a problem. She loves Kai. That boy is a charmer, just like his dad."

Kendra thanked her sister and ended their call, hoping she'd be strong enough to resist Nate's charm this time around.

Chapter 6

Nate climbed the stairs to the small private plane they sometimes chartered for his travel. He got a whiff of a familiar scent. Jasmine with a hint of gardenias.

No, no way.

He removed his shades and stood, stunned, taking in his ex's apologetic expression.

"Guess that answers my question about whether you knew I was coming along." She brushed off her skirt and crossed her legs.

Nate tucked his shades in the inside pocket of his jacket. He stood trying to decide whether or not he'd sit across from Kendra.

He grunted and flopped into his usual seat adjacent to the couch. She seemed relieved he'd chosen to sit across from her.

"No." He held back a few choice names he had for

his brother right now. "Marcus failed to mention it. I realize I screwed up, but I don't appreciate the two of you treating me like a child. I'm a grown-ass man."

"Then start acting like one." Her expression was neutral, her tone unbothered. "Channel your passion for the game in a way that will help your team rather than hurt it. Tap into your desire to win in a way that will motivate your teammates instead of alienating them."

Nate turned to survey the calm waters of the Atlantic Ocean, visible from the window. "Damn. I see we're not pulling punches today."

Kendra smiled sweetly, one long leg crossed over the other and her hands folded in her lap. "You didn't hire me to soothe your ego. You hired me to get results, and that's what you'll get, as long as you stick to the plan."

Nate tried to hold on to the resentment he felt when he realized Marcus had sent Kendra to be his babysitter. That anger was quickly losing ground to the other feeling that grabbed hold of his chest the moment her eyes met his.

Longing.

He wanted her. In his arms. In his bed. In his life. A sentiment he'd fought for the past seven years. Being in such close proximity to the constant object of his affection wasn't helping him win that battle.

Kendra was smart as a whip, sexy as hell and confident in her abilities. Something about that combination made his heart beat faster. That and the expanse of smooth brown skin framed between the hem of her skirt and the top of her leather boots.

Nate raised his hands, his palms facing her. "Relax. I don't plan on going off script again. After all, that's why I'm headed to freaking Montana in the middle of winter, isn't it?" He pulled his jacket closer around him, just thinking of the thirty-degree temperature drop they'd experience once they landed.

She tilted her head, assessing him before responding. "Hopefully, you're also doing it because it's the right thing to do. Wade isn't just your quarterback, he's your friend."

They weren't playing touch football anymore. Kendra had delivered a full-contact, center-mass hit that had knocked him on his ass.

Deservedly so.

She wasn't tiptoeing around his ego. He admired that. Only Kendra Williams could piss him off and make him want her with a single utterance.

It was going to be a rough few days. For him, at least. Kendra seemed unaffected by him. That gave her the upper hand.

He needed to find a way to change that.

Kendra gave herself a mental high five. She stood her ground and told Nate the cold, hard truth while remaining calm, despite the anxiety raging beneath the surface.

Handling Nate with kid gloves wouldn't benefit either of them. Marcus hired her because she'd always been straight with Nate and told him what he needed to hear—whether he wanted to hear it or not. Their painful history aside, she would do just that.

She'd hoped her resolve to be tough with Nate would mitigate her feelings for him. It hadn't. Judging by the half frown that softened the edges of his mouth, a mischievous grin lay just beneath his show of displeasure. So it wasn't deterring him much, either.

Kendra held her poise, despite her increasingly shallow breaths as Nate's gaze raked over her. Heat curled its way up her spine like a black snake climbing a southern red cedar tree in search of prey.

"Of course Wade is my friend, but this is a business," Nate said finally, shifting his gaze out the window for a moment before returning it to her. "Wade understands that more than anyone."

The pilot announced they would take off soon. A growing sense of panic made her limbs feel heavy. She fumbled with her seat belt. It wouldn't catch. They were going to take off and she'd go sailing across the plane.

"Relax. I've got it." Nate knelt in front of her, his large hands covering hers, stilling their movement.

The warmth of his skin penetrated hers and trailed up her arms, her heart beating faster and her breath quickening. Her skin tingled, electricity zipping along her spine.

Even kneeling, Nate's large body loomed over hers. His broad chest and wide shoulders invaded her space as he leaned forward and buckled the seat belt effortlessly.

Nate's gaze met hers and one corner of his mouth curved, his eyes twinkling.

Kendra's hands shook as she inhaled his scent. Her body remembering when last he'd been this close to her on his knees. Her nipples pebbled and a small, inadvertent gasp escaped her mouth.

Nate grinned, then licked his lower lip.

Maybe he was remembering that night, too.

Kendra shut her eyes briefly and exhaled.

No, no, no. This is strictly business. Nothing more.

"Thank you." She settled back against the headrest. "But you'd better get back in your seat."

Nate gave her a knowing grin as he returned to his seat and fastened himself in.

Kendra released a small sigh, missing his nearness, yet thankful for the distance.

"This flight is nearly five hours, and these smaller commuter planes...well, the ride can be a little bumpier than on a commercial flight. You sure you want to do this?"

Kendra nodded in response as she focused on taking long, deep breaths. She wasn't terrified of flying, it just wasn't her preferred mode of travel.

Nothing a rum and Coke or two couldn't resolve.

Only this wasn't a pleasure trip. It was strictly business, and she needed to keep her head clear. That meant toughing it out.

Nate regarded her with apprehension. "Look, I appreciate your commitment, but you don't need to do this. I can handle this on my own, so just say the word and we'll get you off this flight. But I need to know now. *Before* we take off."

"No." Kendra shook her head vehemently. "I'm fine."

"All right." Nate settled back in his seat, his eyes glued to her, as if he expected her head to start spinning.

"I appreciate you looking out for me, despite the fact that you'd rather I not be here."

He shrugged, looking out the window again as the plane taxied down the runway. "Maybe I just didn't want you killing my vibe with your projectile vomiting."

Kendra couldn't help laughing. She dissolved into a fit of giggles that escalated to a laugh so hard it made her belly ache.

Nate laughed, too. He wiped tears from the corners of his eyes. "Better now?"

She stopped laughing long enough to realize that the tense muscles in her back and neck had relaxed. They were airborne and the plane was leveling off. She nodded. "Much. Thank you."

He winked at her. "Good. Now, I assume that in addition to being assigned babysitting duty, you tagged along so we could go over a few things."

She nodded, pulling her portfolio from her bag. "How far outside the box are you willing to go?"

Nate crooked a brow and shifted in his seat, folding his right ankle over his left knee. "What do you mean?"

"A popular home improvement show is looking for a few celebs who want to surprise a family member with a kitchen redo. Marcus suggested they do your mom's kitchen."

"That means my parents would have to be on the show." He ran a hand over his head. "Don't know if I like that. They don't like being in the spotlight."

"Marcus said your mom loves these shows and she's always wanted to be on one." She tapped her pen on her pad. "This is a great opportunity for you to do something fabulous for her, Nate. Something you've always wanted to do. The bonus is it would be great for your image, too."

Nate groaned as he pressed his head against the headrest. "If Marcus thinks Mama will go for it, fine. I'll do it. Anything else?"

"By the end of the day, your brother should have

more info on those guest spots to discuss the play-offs
and a finalized list of media personalities that we'll
pitch additional guest spots to."

"Great. Make sure I get a copy of that list."

"Absolutely." Kendra made another note, then put
her pen and pad away. "Now, about these meetings
with the team and your teammates."

"I don't need you standing next to me like some ven-
triloquist." Nate's tone was tinged with annoyance. "I
know what to say to these guys."

"Great. Then you won't mind running it by me."
Kendra gave Nate a warm smile, but he wasn't buying it. "I'm here to ensure you're prepared for these
meetings and that we stay on message, but I won't be
in any of them. These guys are like your family. It'll
only make things weirder if I'm there."

"Good." He nodded, seemingly relieved.

"Let's just go over the basics of what you plan to
say to Wade. I'll check out a restaurant in town and get
some work done while you meet with him."

"Not going to work."

"Why?"

"There was a change of plans this morning. My
meetings in Memphis were bumped back a couple of
days, so Wade asked me to spend a couple of days with
him and Greer. Thought you knew."

*I'm going to kill Marcus if he has any more sur-
prises up those expensive sleeves of his.*

Unperturbed, Nate composed a text message on his
phone.

Probably to the woman she'd encountered at his
home the day before.

"There must be a hotel or something where I can

stay in town. Shouldn't be terribly difficult to book a room at the last minute in Montana in the middle of winter."

He silently tapped away on his phone.

Good to know you're concerned. She smoothed her skirt and tried not to pout about her ex's lack of interest in her dilemma.

He's your client, not your boyfriend. Get used to it.

"All set." Nate slipped the phone into his pocket.

"You booked me a hotel room?"

"Better. Wade and Greer want you to come to the ranch with me. He and I will chat as soon as we get there. Get all this nonsense out of the way. Then we'll have dinner with them tonight. They also asked us to spend the day with them tomorrow while the older kids are at school."

"Are you sure they don't mind taking on another person? I don't mind staying at a hotel."

Nate gave her a small smile, but sadness lingered in his eyes. "Greer asks about you and Kai all the time. She'll be thrilled to see you."

"It'll be good to see her and Wade again, too. I've always liked them."

He settled back in his chair, his legs crossed again. "Then it's settled."

"Won't your friend Layne be upset about this?"

"Why?" His expression was stoic. She couldn't read him at all.

"So you're saying you two aren't together? Or is your relationship casual and open?" Kendra couldn't help herself. "I'm asking as your media consultant slash publicist, of course."

He chuckled. "Okay, media consultant slash publicist, my relationship with Layne is casual, open and very professional."

Kendra's eyes widened. "You mean she's a—"

"What? Of course not." He laughed. "She's my hot yoga instructor. Sydney recommended her. Layne dated Nick for a while."

"Oh." Kendra pushed a curl back from her forehead. His sister Sydney and her best friend Nick had been roommates for the past few years. "Those two still pretending they're not in love?"

Nate frowned. "They're just friends and roommates. At least, they better be," he added, mumbling under his breath.

"Whatever helps you sleep at night." She couldn't help teasing him. "After all, we started out as best friends, too."

Nate unbuckled his seat belt and sprawled out on the couch. "Yeah, and just look how that turned out." He sighed and dragged a hand down his face. "Sorry, I shouldn't have—"

Kendra waved a hand and shook her head. "I get it. You've always been protective of your baby sister. Just like your twin sister has always been protective of you."

A half grin lit Nate's eyes as he chuckled. "Protective? She acts like she's my mama."

Kendra acknowledged his statement with a small nod. Navia had been furious with her when she broke up with Nate. The rest of the Johnston clan eventually made peace with the situation, but not Navia. She'd probably never forgive her for hurting her twin brother.

"How is Vi doing, anyway? Still calling for my head on a stake?"

Nate grinned. "Nah. She's softened up a little. Now she just wants to see you in stocks for a week or two."

Kendra laughed. "She's warming up to me again. Good to know. And what does she think about this little arrangement?"

He slipped off his expensive leather shoes and shrugged his broad shoulders. "Haven't talked to her about it yet. You know how worked up Vi gets about everything. Marcus and I thought it was best if we waited until we had some viable results to show her."

"Guess I'm not the only one who's afraid of your sister."

"I spent nine months sharing a very small space with Vi." He grinned as he spread a cream-colored cashmere throw over himself. "No one knows better what she's capable of. If I were you, I'd try to wow her."

Kendra pursed her lips. Nate was teasing her. Didn't mean she wouldn't check underneath her car seat for ticking devices—just in case.

Chapter 7

"Hello, Nate." Greer Willis gave him an awkward hug—unlike the dozens she'd given him before. "Wade'll be here shortly. He picked Jake and Mariah up from school."

Greer's demeanor was pleasant, but the narrowing of her blue eyes and the sharp pronunciation of his name—without any of the soft edges of her deep Southern accent—sufficiently conveyed her indignation.

She was sweet and cordial, but also fiercely protective of her family. An endearing quality when he wasn't on the wrong side of it.

Today, he clearly was.

"Kendra!" An authentic smile lit Greer's face, highlighting her natural beauty. She wrapped Kendra in a tight embrace. "Honey, it's so good to see you. Hasn't been the same without you."

"Good to see you, too, Greer. I can't wait to see the kids. How old are they?"

Greer threaded her arm through Kendra's, leading her to the living room. "Jake is ten and Mariah is eight. They've grown like weeds since you saw them last. Noah is three and baby Allie is thirteen months. The little ones are down for a nap. You'll see them soon enough. Can I get y'all something?"

"No, thank you. We're good." Kendra surveyed the impressive house. The architectural gem was made up mostly of local fieldstone, walls of glass and a symphony of light-colored woods. "My God, Greer, this place is gorgeous. The architecture…and those views. It's stunning."

Greer's grin widened and her cheeks colored. She was still a small-town Alabama girl who grew up on a working farm, never imagining a charmed life. It was one of the reasons Nate had always genuinely liked and respected her. Greer and Wade were good, down-to-earth folks. His friends.

He'd hurt them both.

"Still can't believe we get to wake up here every day." A strand of Greer's wavy honey-blond hair escaped her low ponytail. She tucked it behind her ear. "I'll show you around when the little ones wake. Meantime, have a seat. I'll ask Edison to fetch y'all's bags and take 'em to the guesthouse."

"There's a guesthouse?" Kendra eased onto the large gray sectional. It blended nicely with maple flooring stained the same shade of gray as the driftwood that washed ashore on the beach back home. Kendra laughed. "What am I thinking? Of course there's a guesthouse. How much land do you have here?"

"'Bout a hundred acres. We'll take you for a tour tomorrow, when there's plenty of daylight."

Chest burning and his mouth dry, Nate paced behind the sofa rather than taking a seat.

Until he saw the anguish that dulled Greer's blue eyes, he hadn't considered the collateral damage he'd caused.

"Greer, I'm sorry I got you caught up in this." The words blurted from his mouth.

"I know you are, Nate. But it's a bell you can't unring." She shrugged. "Who knows, maybe somethin' good'll come out of all of this after all. Now, have a seat, please. You're making me nervous as a long-tailed cat in a room full of rocking chairs, pacing like that."

Nate took a seat on the other side of Kendra and massaged the tension in his neck. He stayed quiet, responding only to direct questions from Greer and Kendra as they caught up.

The baby monitor alerted Greer that Noah and Allie were up from their naps. She excused herself and stepped away.

Nate released a long breath when Greer left the room.

"Harder facing them than you expected?" Kendra leaned closer, her tone compassionate and her expression thoughtful.

"I was so focused on how this whole thing impacted my life, my career..." Nate raked his fingers through his hair, trying to quell the guilt gnawing at his gut as he imagined how disappointed Jake and Mariah must have been at his remarks about their father. Wade was their hero. "I didn't think about how my words must have hurt Greer and the kids or Tyree's mom—Ms. Eleanor. People I know and respect."

"That's why you're here, to smooth things out." Kendra's voice was reassuring as she placed a hand on his knee to still it. "If they weren't interested in repairing the relationship, they wouldn't have invited you to stay overnight."

Nate found comfort in the warmth from Kendra's hand seeping into his skin through the layer of fabric between them. She'd always had a calming effect on him; the perfect balance to his fiery personality.

"Take a deep breath and relax. Be honest with Wade about why you said what you did, and about how you feel, knowing you've hurt him."

Nate heaved a sigh. He didn't come here to grovel. He hadn't asked for this situation, and nothing he said that night was news to anyone inside the Marauders organization.

He boarded that plane expecting it would all be so simple. He'd lay out the facts and apologize for talking publicly about team business—even if he hadn't intended to.

Experiencing Greer's anguish firsthand…suddenly it didn't feel so simple.

"Nate, good of you to come all this way."

Nate and Kendra turned toward Wade. He stood in the doorway, each arm draped around a child. His thin smile hovered at the surface, not reaching his wary brown eyes.

"Thanks for seeing me, Wade, and for inviting us to stay." Nate stood, his gut churning as he crossed the room to shake his quarterback's hand. He stooped so his towering frame was closer to the children's height. "Jake, Mariah, you've both gotten so big."

Neither child responded. They stared at him blankly. Mariah drew closer to her father like Nate was the Big Bad Wolf, rather than her beloved "Uncle Nate." Her reaction hit him like a body slam on Astroturf.

"Say hello to Uncle Nate and Ms. Kendra." Wade squeezed their shoulders.

They mumbled their hellos. Mariah's eyes brimmed with heartache; Jake's glowed with animus.

Wade dispatched the kids to wash their hands and faces before their after-school snack. Then he crossed the room and pulled Kendra into a bear hug, inducing a fleeting moment of envy that heated Nate's face. Wade's Texas accent deepened. "Lemme borrow Nate for a bit."

"Of course." Kendra waved a hand.

Wade flashed his trademark smile. The one plastered on no less than half a dozen glossy magazines each year. "Greer will be down with the kids in a sec. And don't worry, I promise to bring 'im back in one piece."

"Have a seat." Wade closed the doors to his office. The walls were covered with well-worn shiplap. Mounted antlers hung over the roaring fireplace and rainbow trout replicas flanked either side. Faux animal rugs accented the space.

"Beer?" Wade opened a large wooden console that concealed a drink cooler.

"Thanks." Nate sank into the metal-studded brown leather couch broken in over the years.

Wade pulled out two domestic beers, popped the

tops and handed him one. He sank onto a large cushioned chair. "All right, Nate. You traveled twenty-four hundred miles so we could talk man-to-man. You got my undivided attention."

Nate took a long drag of his beer, then set the bottle on a coaster hewn from tree bark.

"I can't tell you how sorry I am about this. Not just to you, but to Greer and the kids. Didn't mean for any of this to happen. It's not my style. You know that."

Wade nodded thoughtfully. "'Preciate that, Nate, but the story's out there now. Nothing either of us can do about it."

"Believe me, I'd do anything to take that entire night back."

"Bet you would. Them pretty little things caused you a lot of trouble. Hope you got a helluva night out of it." Wade chuckled bitterly, referring to the two young women who'd cornered Nate in the VIP section, gotten him riled up again about the loss and recorded his rant.

"Didn't sleep with either of them. I was so amped and more than a little drunk." Nate's face grew hot, thinking of how the blonde and her friend manipulated him. How he stupidly played right into their hands. "About what I said—"

"You meant every word. Just didn't mean for it to go public." Wade took a healthy swig of his light beer and set the bottle down. He leaned forward, his elbows on his knees. "I know. You been telling me as much for a while now. If I'd listened earlier, maybe we'd still be in this thing with a shot at winning it all."

Nate stood, pacing in front of the fireplace. "We all had a hand in it." He jerked a thumb toward himself. "My screwups cost us big."

"Kind of you to own up to your part, Nate, but the truth is, those throws weren't crisp and my timing was off. You wouldn't have dropped them if I'd done my job right. I was scrambling, anticipating another hit."

So that was it. Wade's heart hadn't been in the game for the entire season. Nate thought Wade had resigned himself to never winning the big one. That he was just riding out the remainder of his contract. Instead, he was afraid of taking another hit like the one that leveled him near the end of the previous season. He'd suffered a concussion and two broken ribs.

Wade's performance dropped off considerably when he returned. Two years ago, he was one of the top quarterbacks in the league. He could be again.

"All those times I rode you for not being focused… why didn't you tell me the truth?"

"Who's gonna trust a QB who admits he's scared to take another hard hit? Besides, saying it out loud meant admitting it to myself. For me, that was worse than everyone else knowing."

Nate sank onto the sofa. What could he say?

He'd taken bad hits in his career. Suffered injuries that still nagged him, reminding him the sand was running out in the hourglass of his pro football career. The first few games back were always hard. He was unsure of the injured body part—an ankle and later a knee. Then there was the fear of getting reinjured. For him, it was mind over matter. He focused on his goal: winning a championship. He could spend his retirement resting and nursing his aching joints.

"Look, I know you probably don't want to hear this, but the Marauders work with a sports psychologist. Maybe—"

"Already tried that." Wade stood suddenly, agitated. He got two more beers from the fridge, opened them and placed one in front of Nate.

"You've already been to Dr. Mays?"

"Didn't want the team to know I was having panic attacks. My first game back, this big-ass defensive end came at me and I broke into a cold sweat. Heart beating a mile a minute. Happened again in the next game and the next. Went to an independent sports psychologist."

"Did it help?" Nate gripped his bottle, fully aware of the answer, based on the distressed look on his friend's face.

"I'm fighting my natural self-preservation instincts every time I step onto that field. Told myself time and again it's all in my head. That I can get past it." Wade shrugged again. "But short of taking antianxiety drugs, nothing seems to help. If I gotta drug up just to do my job…maybe it ain't the right job for me anymore."

"You're not thinking about retiring, are you?" It hurt that he was the reason Wade was considering walking away from the game they loved.

"Not like I need the money." Wade nodded toward the wall of glass at the far end of the room with its view of the mountains and a pristine lake. "We've been smart. Saved. Invested. I was trying to hold out and fulfill the final two years of my contract, but maybe it's time to pack it up and walk away." Wade was matter-of-fact about the prospect, as if he'd already resigned himself to it.

"There has to be another answer. We'll make adjustments. Work harder. I got a hand on those passes, so I should've been able to haul them in and hold on to them, simple as that."

Wade met Nate's gaze. "Or maybe you were right all along. Time for me to walk away."

"I *never* said that."

"Been in the league ten years, Nate. It's been a good ride, but that's a hell of a long time. I don't want to be one of those guys who can't enjoy his life by the time he walks away."

They sat in silence as Nate wrestled with what to say to shovel himself out of the six-foot-deep ditch he'd dug and dragged his team into.

"You talk to Greer about this?"

"She's thrilled that I'd be here year-round to help with the kids. She's put her life on hold so I could live my dream. Maybe it's time I support hers. She has a couple of business ideas. Stuff she's been talking about a long time. Maybe it's my turn to be her cheerleader."

Nate assessed his friend, who didn't seem enthused about the prospect. "I know Greer would love to have you home, but what did she say when you told her you were considering retiring?"

Wade chuckled softly. "She said Willises don't run scared. We stay and fight."

Nate laughed, too. "*That* sounds like the Greer Willis I know. I'm just thankful she didn't meet me at the door with a shotgun rather than one of those Hollywood hugs."

"Not gon' lie, she was madder than a hornet when she saw that video." Wade took another swig of his beer. "I hid her phone for two days to keep her from calling you and telling you off."

"I deserved it." Nate gripped his beer, raising his

eyes to Wade's. "What about Jake and Mariah? Don't think I've ever felt like as much of an ass as I did seeing myself through their eyes today."

"You're their Uncle Nate. So yeah, they're pretty upset. Jake's angry. Mariah's feelings are hurt."

Nate drained the remainder of his first beer. He took a gulp of the second. "If it's okay with you and Greer, I'd like to apologize to them. I won't push," he added quickly, in response to the concern in Wade's eyes. "But I want them to know how sorry I am."

Wade nodded solemnly. "I'll talk to Greer about it. If she doesn't have a problem with it, neither do I."

"Thanks," Nate said quietly. "And about you retiring… I know I have no right to ask, but I wish you'd reconsider."

"Oz will be just fine. The kid's good. Really good. Better than me," Wade said, referring to Osgood Wells—the Marauders' backup quarterback who'd been playing behind Wade for the past three seasons. "He went 3 and 1 when I got hurt last year. You said yourself the kid is star material."

"And I still say he's star material." Nate smirked. "But he ain't a star. Not yet. He could use a mentor in his ear helping him along."

"Been doing that the past three years."

"Yeah, but the past three years he was also your competition. Maybe now you'll teach him some of the tricks you've been holding back."

Wade sipped his beer thoughtfully, not denying that mentoring Oz had been the last thing on his mind these past three years. "I'll think about it. But as for us…this thing is over as far as I'm concerned. You're a good friend, Nate. Don't see the need to talk about this again."

Nate's shoulders relaxed as he reached across the table to shake his friend's hand.

Chapter 8

Kendra bounced little Allie on her lap. The infant cooed and giggled, blowing spit bubbles.

"She's adorable." Kendra kissed the girl's round cheek. Inhaled her irresistible, baby scent. "All the kids are, and they're so well-mannered."

"Told you I was lucky." Greer grinned, cutting three turkey sandwiches into triangles for the children.

"No, you're a good mom. Wade and the kids are lucky to have you."

"Thanks." Greer stacked the sandwich triangles on plates and set them on the table. She sighed. "God, I miss having you there whenever I'm in Memphis. You were the one person whose intentions I never doubted. I always felt like we would've been friends even if Wade and Nate weren't."

"Me, too." Kendra smiled, rearranging little Allie's headband. "You were my favorite, hands down."

Greer poured apple juice into acrylic tumblers. "I'm thrilled you and Nate are back together. Sure, I'm a little miffed with him now, but he's always been a good friend to me and Wade. Broke my heart to see how miserable he's been without you and Kai."

"We're not back together." A knot tightened in Kendra's throat. She shifted Allie on her lap, steering the infant away from the gold hoop she was trying to rip from her ear. "I'm his media consultant."

Greer put the juice away and set the cups and plates on the kitchen table. She turned to Kendra. "You do realize he's still in love with you?"

Without waiting for a response, Greer called the children down for their snack.

It was just as well. Greer's words left her head spinning.

The attraction was still there. That was evident from the way he'd scanned her figure on more than one occasion. But was it possible he still loved her?

The resentment on Nate's face when he first laid eyes on her at the restaurant and his aggravation with her when they met at the beach house suggested otherwise.

The one-night stands they'd had were products of their lingering chemistry, bottled-up frustrations and close proximity, not love.

Greer took Allie, who was reaching for her. She settled the girl on her lap, tied on her pink bib and fed her green baby food out of a chunky plastic spoon. "Thinking about what I said?"

Kendra watched Jake, Mariah and Noah nibbling their sandwiches and drinking apple juice. "No, I was wondering what you're feeding Allie. Looks like strained peas, but it smells better than any baby food I remember."

Greer grinned. "It's one of the baby food formulas I've been working on. Allie here is my personal guinea pig."

"She doesn't seem to mind. In fact, I've never seen a baby so enthusiastic about eating her vegetables." Kendra nodded toward the infant, who happily consumed the strained peas, some of which now dotted her chin. "Is this just for Allie or are you thinking of going commercial?"

Greer's eyes lit up. "Been thinking of starting my own baby food company. Everything will be fresh and organic—shipped right to your door. I want to start it as soon as Wade retires."

"What does Wade think?"

"He's been so supportive. He insists I don't need to wait for him to retire, but I'd like at least one of us to be focused on the kids."

"If Allie's enthusiasm is any indication, you've got a hit on your hands."

"Oh my gosh." Greer looked down at her daughter, who evidently wasn't satisfied with the speed at which her mother was feeding her. She dipped her chunky little fingers into the bowl and sucked strained peas from her fingers, getting it all over her face and in her nose. Greer grabbed a wipe and cleaned Allie's hands and face. "I'm excited about the possibility, but I'm scared to death by it, too. You must understand that."

"I do." Kendra took the dirty wipes from Greer and tossed them in the trash. "Never more than when I agreed to take Nate on as a client."

"Let me guess, it was Marcus's idea." Greer grinned as she resumed feeding Allie.

"How'd you know?"

"Had a feeling." Greer shrugged, her Alabama twang evident. "He's an old romantic soul like me and Wade. We been praying you two would figure out you were meant to be together."

"I hate to disappoint all of you, but this arrangement is strictly business."

"Got yourself convinced of that, don't you?" Greer shook her head. "You don't want to tell me? That's fine. But if you're lying to yourself…well, that's another matter altogether."

"What are you talking about?" Kendra tamped down the irritation rising in her chest.

"Isn't it obvious?" She smiled sweetly. "You're still in love with him, too."

Kendra glanced toward the sound of Nate's and Wade's voices approaching. She pointed a finger at Greer. "No more of this me-and-Nate-getting-back-together talk."

"Fine." Greer grinned, spooning more peas into Allie's mouth. "But it's gon' make y'all's sleeping arrangements mighty awkward."

"You mean to tell me this huge guesthouse only has one bedroom?" Kendra stood in the living room, her arms folded.

"There's another bedroom, but we're renovating it. The furniture's gone and there are ladders and paint buckets everywhere." Wade ran a hand through his longish brown hair, which dusted the collar of his suede jacket. "Honest."

Kendra propped a hand on her hip as she surveyed the space. "The sofa looks comfy enough. Got any extra blankets?"

"Sure thing." He gave Nate an apologetic stare. "I'll grab 'em for you."

"Look, it's my fault," Nate said. "I should've been clearer when I explained you were coming along. Didn't think about it because I knew the guesthouse has two bedrooms. I'll take the sofa."

"I'll be fine here." Kendra raised a hand before he could launch into his objection. "End of discussion."

Kendra sank into the bubbles threatening to spill over the side of the old claw-foot tub and sighed. She inhaled the yummy candles perched on the window ledge, which provided the only light in the room. The mingled scent of cranberry and orange wafted through the space, calming her frazzled nerves. She stared up through the skylight, admiring the stars dotting the sky.

Just a few more days. I can handle this.

She repeated the words in her head because the truth was, she didn't know if she could handle spending this much time with Nate. Especially after what Greer had said.

You do realize he's still in love with you? You're still in love with him, too.

Kendra dunked her head beneath the water, holding her breath a few seconds before emerging. Maybe that would disrupt the rogue thoughts of Nate Johnston roaming around the guesthouse barely dressed.

She wiped the water from her face and sat up, pressing her back to the still-cool cast-iron tub as she hugged her knees to her chest.

Concentrate on the job. Nate is just another client.
This was business. She was helping Nate and advancing her career. In fact, over dinner, Greer asked her to consider taking her on as a client once she got the baby food company up and running.

She'd planned to move her consultancy to exclusively serve athletes, but Greer was more than just a potential client. She was a friend. Besides, Kendra believed in what Greer was doing. Having tasted a few of the samples herself, she'd be crazy not to consider it.

There was a light tap at the door. Kendra froze, wrapping her arms tighter around her knees. "Yes?"

"Kai wants to say good-night."

"It's not even eight. I'll call him back as soon as I'm out of the tub."

"It's nearly ten there," Nate reminded her.

She sighed, making sure all of her essential parts were shielded by the bubbles. "The door isn't locked." Another apparent casualty of the remodeling. "Come in."

Light from the hall spilled into the room as Nate stepped inside wearing fitted jeans that hugged his bottom and a tight gray athletic shirt that outlined the hard-earned muscles of his chest and biceps. He handed Kendra his cell phone, then stood back against the door frame, his eyes roving anywhere in the room except on her.

"Kai Kai. How are you?"

"Good. When are you and Daddy coming home?"

"As soon as we can, sweetie. We're in Montana with Uncle Wade and Aunt Greer."

"You know them, too?" Kai had been with his dad whenever he visited with Wade and his family.

"Since before you were born." She smiled. "Auntie Greer's an old friend."

"Are Jake and Mariah there? Does Jake still have his train set?" Kai's voice rose with excitement.

"They're not here with me now. I'm…we're in the guesthouse. But yes, he still has his train. Are you being a good boy for Nana?"

"Yes."

"Did you brush your teeth before bed?"

"Yes, Mommy." He sighed. "I always brush my teeth before bed."

"Good. Now, no more stalling. Go to sleep."

She bid Kai a final good-night, blew a kiss through the phone, then handed it to Nate. "Thank you. I hate not tucking him in tonight. I would've been so disappointed if I'd forgotten to call him before bed."

Nate frowned, his mood suddenly surly. He shoved his phone into his back pocket. "I'll let you get back to your bath."

He left, closing the door behind him.

Kendra sank beneath the water, her eyes readjusting to the candlelit room.

What the hell was that about?

Chapter 9

Nate trudged back to the master bedroom, undressed and hopped in the large, rugged, stacked-stone-and-glass shower.

He lathered himself, gritting his teeth as he recalled Kendra's words. She was distraught over missing a single night tucking Kai in.

Welcome to my world, princess.

Most nights he had to settle for wishing Kai good-night by phone, as he had tonight. Did she have any clue how much it tore at him that he seldom got to tuck his own son into bed at night?

Kai was growing up so fast. Already six years old, soon he'd be too old for bedtime stories and good-night kisses. And he was missing all of it. Moments he'd never get back.

He'd witnessed his son's first words and first steps

via a video recording. He didn't want to miss out on any more milestones in Kai's life, but Kendra hadn't given him much choice.

The steaming hot water sluiced over his skin, relaxing his tired muscles and aching joints.

Wade was right; the game had taken a toll on their bodies. He wasn't as fast as he'd been a few seasons ago when he was so explosive he could outrun every cornerback in the league in a footrace to the end zone.

He never imagined retiring without hoisting that trophy over his head at least once. The Marauders were close to reaching the next level. They just needed a few tweaks to the defense and a couple more offensive weapons. He couldn't throw in the towel when they were so damn close.

Nights like this, when he was missing the goofy grin and contagious laughter of his son, he gave fleeting consideration to the prospect of retiring sooner rather than later.

Nate shook off the thought. He had a plan. Two more years, then he was out. This wasn't just about him; it was about securing the future of his family and his foundation.

He toweled off and slipped on his underwear. After a few minutes of scanning channels, Nate turned off the television and dropped to the floor to do push-ups.

How the hell had he managed to be mad at, grateful to and turned on by one woman, all at the same time?

Kendra.

He groaned, gritting his teeth as he switched to one-armed push-ups, not caring that he'd need another shower if he kept this up.

All day he'd kept his attraction to her in check—

despite the fact that she looked good enough to pour in a glass and serve on ice in that body-hugging gray pencil skirt and knee-high boots. In spite of the electricity humming along the surface of his skin when she'd placed her hand on his, comforting him. But seeing her in the tub with her slick brown skin and wet curls—that was more than any man could be expected to handle.

He'd tried to distract himself by counting the bathroom tiles and studying every feature of that damn bathroom like he'd have a pop quiz on it the next morning. Still, his eyes roamed back to her in that tub again and again. Fortunately, she'd been too busy talking to Kai to notice.

Nate slipped on his flannel pajama bottoms and slippers, then padded to the kitchen for a snack. He opened the fridge and smiled. Wade and Greer had stocked it with leftovers.

Nate cut a few slices of ham, then added some macaroni and cheese and green bean casserole to his plate before heating it in the microwave.

"What smells so good?"

Nate turned, startled by Kendra moving toward him in purple pajamas. Her damp curls were wrapped in a white turban.

"Leftovers." He turned back to the microwave to watch the timer count down.

She shoved a few items into her luggage, then inched closer. "I shouldn't be eating this late—but now I'm hungry again. Any more?"

Arms folded, he tipped his head toward the fridge. "Plenty."

Kendra cocked her head to the side, her brow furrowed. She opened the fridge. "Thanks."

She made her plate in silence as he waited for his to finish heating.

Nate removed his plate from the microwave, grabbed his utensils and headed back to his room. He needed to put space between them, get a good night's rest and let his annoyance subside.

"Wait." Kendra's plea halted him. "Have I done something to upset you? Everything seemed fine, then suddenly I'm getting grunts and one-word answers."

"Everything is fine, Kendra. I'm tired, and I'd like to go to bed, if that's all right."

She shrugged. "You don't want to talk about it? Fine. But if I've somehow pissed you off, you should at least be mature enough to tell me what I did wrong."

"Like you were when you packed your bags and took off seven years ago?" He swung around. "That the kind of maturity you're talking about?"

Kendra lowered her gaze. "I didn't know exactly how to handle what I was feeling."

"I was prepared to spend my life with you, and you gave me the 'it's not you, it's me' speech. You said the life you would've had with me wasn't the one you envisioned for yourself. Do you have any idea how that made me feel?" Nate put the plate on the table and clenched his fist.

"Shitty," he supplied when she didn't respond. "Everything I'd done up to then was so that I could give you the life you deserved."

Head tilted, her brow creased. "That's sweet, Nate, but I never asked you to take care of me. I'm fully capable of caring for myself."

"I know, but…" Nate ran a hand through his hair and huffed. "All those years I watched your mom struggle to support you and Dash, working long hours and still managing to be a good mother. Most days she was tired to the bone. Apologizing because she couldn't be at your brother's track meets or your school plays. I didn't want that for you. For us. I wanted to give you everything. Anything you wanted."

"What I wanted was to have a relationship *and* a career. I wanted to do what I loved during the day and go home to the person I loved at night, just like you did. But you couldn't cope with that, as if it infringed upon your manhood."

"I didn't object to your career. I just didn't want you working with random athletes."

"Why?" She stepped closer.

"You know how those guys are. Chasing skirts. Going after anything pretty that moves."

"Exactly." Kendra's self-satisfied expression said it all. He'd justified her reasons for walking away.

His cheeks flushed with heat. "C'mon, Kendra, you know what I meant. Not every guy is like that. I'm not."

"Okay." She shrugged. "Let's look at the most essential point. You didn't trust me."

"Now you're turning this on me? You're the one who walked away because you didn't trust me."

"And you sabotaged my career because you didn't trust that I could deal with your colleagues without ending up in their beds."

They were both silent, stewing over the unhealed wounds they'd inflicted on each other.

Nate inhaled deeply, then released his breath slowly. He shook his head. "For the record, I did trust you. Just

ope Kai

creased
ressed
o hold

Liam
nd he

very
path
e's
…
n-

ourself in a bad situation. Be-
e of what I'd do if one of those
on you. Figured it'd be safer if
out. I didn't realize how impor-
ntil it was too late."

talked to me instead of trying to lay
e you were the sheriff in a one-horse
ers of her eyes were damp. "Like what
t matter."

ed her face. "I was wrong, and I'm sorry.
ld take it back and do it all over again."

." Kendra swiped a finger beneath her eye;
quavered. "The choice I made…it was a mis-
e we all ended up paying for."

had waited a long time to hear those words. For
mation that what they'd shared was real.

shouldn't have brought it up." His fists were
ed at his sides as he resisted the urge to take her
his arms.

She sniffled, raising her eyes, wet with tears, to his. "And I shouldn't have made such a big deal about not being able to tuck Kai in tonight. That's what upset you, isn't it? I was complaining about one night without him while you…" She sighed heavily. "While you're away from him most nights."

Nate shrugged, watching a line of dark clouds rolling in and lightning in the distance.

"Every day I regret the pain my choice has caused both you and Kai." Kendra touched his arm. She leaned into him when he didn't respond. "I know it's a lot to ask, but I hope that one day you can forgive me. Both you and Kai."

His chest ached from the pain and regret he saw

in her brown eyes. "What do you mean you
will forgive you?"

Kendra's eyebrows gathered and a deep line
her forehead, hardening her soft features. She
her lips together tightly, as if she were trying
back a sob.

"He's been asking for you a lot more since
came into our lives. He sees Liam with the girls a
doesn't understand why his dad isn't in his life e
day." Her voice grew faint; the tears etched a salty
down her face faster than she could erase them. "H
only six now, but eventually he'll be hurt and angry
he'll hate me for taking him away from his dad." Ke
dra covered her mouth and turned away.

Nate wrapped his arms around her, pulling her we
cheek to his bare chest. He kissed her forehead. "Ka
adores you. He could never stay angry with you. He's
too much of a mama's boy."

Kendra laughed against his chest, then pulled away
enough to meet his gaze. "Like his dad?"

He held her at arm's length. "Whoa? Me? A mama's
boy?"

She raised an eyebrow and punched him in the gut
playfully. "Uh…yeah."

Nate peeked through his thumb and forefinger.
"Maybe just a tad. Nothing wrong with that."

"No, there isn't." Kendra smiled wistfully. "There's
a little mama's boy in every good man."

He pulled her to him again, his body reacting to the
exquisite sensation of her curves pressed against him.
"You saying I'm a good man?"

"I wouldn't be here now if I didn't believe you are.
That's why this campaign is so important. I want peo-

ple to see the kind, brilliant man I've always known. That's my mission. Once we accomplish that, everything else will come. The contract, the endorsements."

"Didn't think you believed in me anymore." He paused, his next words catching in his throat. "That's what hurt most when you left."

Kendra dropped her stare, but Nate cupped her chin, raising her eyes to meet his again.

"I know that you don't want to talk about this and that what's done is done. But in all these years, it's never felt over to me. There's always been a tiny piece of me that—despite the anger and hurt feelings—still wanted you to be there for me like you are right now."

She tried to pull away, but he held on tight, his gaze not leaving hers.

"I need to know, is there still a chance we can be a family?"

Yes.

That single word hung at the back of her throat, unable to make its way past her lips. She shook her head, trying to clear the warm thoughts that were fogging her brain and spreading throughout her body. Making her want things she had no right to. "Nate, I—"

He leaned down and kissed her open mouth, midsentence. His strong arms encircling her waist, he pulled their lower bodies together.

Kendra gasped at the sensation of his lips pressed to hers. She savored the taste and warmth of his mouth as she melted into his strong embrace. The memories of what they'd once been filled her body with heat and caused a delicious ache in her nipples and between her thighs.

Kissing Nate went against every rule she'd established when she agreed to take him on as a client. Rules she put in place to safeguard their working relationship and protect her heart.

Despite the blissful contentment she felt, surrendering to the magnetic pull between them, she needed to put a stop to it and regain control. Kendra pressed the heels of her hands into his chest, but Nate pulled her closer. Kissed her more fervently.

The logical objections her brain posed gave way to the temptation and desire that made her skin tingle. She relaxed into him and pressed her fingers to the warm skin of his muscular back.

She missed the strength of his hands, the tenderness of his kiss. The way his touch filled her belly with fire and made her knees weak.

Her senses were overloaded with the heat emanating from his skin, the scent of his freshly scrubbed skin, mingled with a hint of sweat and the salty taste of him.

Maybe she was overly cautious. They'd done this before—had one night together and then sensibly walked away.

Would it be so wrong if we did it again?

But that wasn't what Nate had proposed. He'd asked whether they could be a family.

That, she couldn't promise.

Kendra pulled away, her eyes searching his. "Nate, please, we agreed to keep this strictly business."

Nate sighed heavily, frowning. He cupped her cheek with his rough palm. "*We* didn't agree to anything. You insisted on it."

"I know, but you promised to keep your hands to yourself." She poked a finger in his chest, attempting to lighten the suddenly heavy mood. The tension between them was finally abating. She couldn't afford for things to go back to the way they were.

"We both made promises." He dropped his gaze, his voice gruff. "Things change."

He didn't need to elaborate. Kendra knew exactly what he meant. The night they'd gotten tossed from the prom, they spent the night on Pleasure Cove Beach, watching the waves crash on the shore. He'd made love to her on the beach under an incredible full moon and a sky full of stars that had never shone brighter.

That night, Nate promised to always love her. She'd promised the same.

They were just kids. Neither of them had a clue what life had in store or how they'd change.

Kendra clenched her fists at her side and sank her teeth into her lower lip as she searched for the right words.

Head cocked to the side, Nate's dark eyes studied hers. His words were a husky whisper that sent electricity up her spine. "There's obviously still something between us."

"We have a lot of history and an amazing little boy. It's hard not to get caught up in those feelings."

"Then maybe we should explore them." He trailed the back of his hand down the side of her face. "See where this thing takes us."

Kendra fought off the overwhelming desire to let Nate take her back to his bed and make love to her. His mouth exploring hers, his hands roaming her skin as she lay in his arms.

Sex and business don't mix. Stay strong.

"Wanting each other isn't enough, Nate." She

stepped back, giving herself room to breathe in air that wasn't permeated with his fresh, woodsy scent. "And what we want isn't necessarily what's best for us. No matter how badly we want it."

Nate caught her hand as she turned to walk away, tugging her toward him again. "I don't believe our being together isn't what's best for us or Kai. Neither do you."

"One kiss and you're talking about being a family? I can't promise you that."

Nate groaned, releasing her hand. "We're not kids on a first date, Kendra. We know each other. Most important, we love our son and want what's best for him."

Kendra wanted Nate. Loved him. But did he love her? Or was this just about finally making them a family?

Nate grew up in a big, close family that had earned the moniker "the black Waltons." His parents had been married for four decades. Nate wanted Kai to be raised by both his parents—just as he'd been.

She wanted that, too, but not at the expense of a one-sided marriage where they were just in it for the kids. Relationships like that didn't last.

Her parents were proof of that.

"We both want what's best for Kai. That's why we need to focus on the mission at hand. There's a lot on the line here, Nate. Your career, your future income, the work you've been able to do with the foundation—"

"Your career." His mouth tugged down in a frown. "It's serious, I get it, but *this*—" he gestured between them "—is important, too."

She lifted her chin and met his condemning gaze. "This isn't the time to explore the past. Not with so much at stake for both of us."

"Fine." He gathered his plate, turning to leave.

Kendra grabbed his elbow. "That doesn't mean we can't sit down and have a meal together."

"You want to keep this thing strictly business? Well, I don't usually have shirtless midnight business meetings." He narrowed his gaze, his tone icy.

"You give interviews in the locker room when you're half-dressed. How is this any different?"

"You know why it's different." Nate put the plate down again. "What is it that you want from me, Kendra?"

She stood stunned, her mouth slack, unable to reply.

"I ask you to marry me and you walk away. Just when I think I'm finally over it, you find some way to mess with my head again. I just wanted to have a quiet late-night snack in my room. *Alone.* But you couldn't let it be." His words came in quick, angry bursts. "I kiss you. Tell you I want to be with you and Kai. You say I'm pushing too hard. But, oh, by the way, why don't we sit down for a nice, civil business meal in our pajamas?"

Her stomach clenched and her hands shook. He was right. She was being selfish—trying to hold on to him while maintaining her distance. "I'm sorry. I don't know exactly how to do this. I want us to be friends again. Not just because we're working together or even because of Kai. We were friends long before we dated. I miss that."

Nate shook his head. "After everything we've been through, I can't just be friends. Maybe someday, but not tonight."

Kendra bit her lower lip, concentrating on the superficial physical pain rather than the deep ache in her heart as he walked away.

Chapter 10

Nate dropped his luggage by the front door and stumbled to the couch. They'd landed in Memphis later than expected.

Good to finally be home again.

He dropped Kendra off at a nearby hotel and headed to his place.

He had plenty of room to put her up for the night. But after the night they'd shared at Wade and Greer's guesthouse, they both agreed it would be better if she stayed at a hotel.

Nate just wanted a cold beer and a hot bath before what would surely be a grueling day.

First, there was the meeting with the team. Then he would meet with a couple of his teammates. After he made his personal amends to everyone on the list— except Tyree and Dade, who were still dodging his calls—he'd take to the podium in a press conference at the team facilities.

Nate made his way to the fridge. He tossed out a couple of suspect take-out containers, then pulled out a bottle of imported beer. He settled on the couch again when the doorbell rang.

His neighbor collected his mail when he was away, and was always a little too eager to bring over his mail and newspapers. Nate opened the door.

"Hello, Nate. Miss me?"

Stephanie Weiss—the devil herself and the cause of this entire fiasco—lifted her head, her face previously shielded by her large-brimmed hat. Her mouth curved in a sly grin.

"What the hell are you doing here?" He gritted out the words between clenched teeth.

"Got a proposal for you." She smiled sweetly, glancing over his shoulder. "May I come in?"

"Not if your ass was on fire and I had the only bucket of water for thirty miles," he seethed. "You've got five seconds before I call security to haul you out of here."

She seemed slightly irritated by his rebuff, but mostly amused. "Fine. Then I'll save my questions for the press conference tomorrow. Just thought you'd welcome the opportunity to sit down and explain your side of things."

"Sit down with the devil who caused this whole shit storm? No thanks." He crossed his arms. "Yeah, I know it was you who sent those girls to ambush me."

She smirked. "Now that's just unsubstantiated speculation." Stephanie echoed the words he'd used in the press conference he had three years ago, when he'd distanced himself from her after the scandal broke.

"Is that what this is about?" He placed a hand high on the doorjamb as he leaned against the frame. "You're still pissed because I wouldn't help you ruin my friend's career?"

"You didn't have any qualms about ruining mine." She narrowed her eyes, the irises the color of muddy water, and pressed her thin lips into a tight line. "This time, I had indisputable proof, and it's you who came out looking like the fool."

Nate clenched his fist and gritted his teeth. Swallowed back all the things he wanted to say to this woman. Things his mama would whup his behind for if she heard him utter them in mixed company. "Get off my property. Now. Believe me, I'd enjoy watching the cops drag you out of here."

Stephanie shrugged, then flipped her shoulder-length dark hair. "Fine, but I came here to offer a truce. Give me an exclusive interview before your press conference tomorrow, and I'll back off. Let this thing die down."

Nate laughed bitterly. "Be a clown in the circus you created? No thanks."

"What are you worried about? You'll come out smelling like a rose. You always do."

"I'll take option two." His patience was gone. "Now, get the fuck off my property."

"War it is then." Stephanie grinned, tying the belt of her red wool coat. She turned and walked away, calling over her shoulder, "Don't say I didn't give you a chance to end this thing peacefully."

Nate slammed the door and pressed his back to it, running his fingers through his hair. He'd screwed himself over big-time when he'd messed around with her.

Aside from letting Kendra walk away, getting with Stephanie Weiss was his biggest regret.

His friends had warned him that breaking a big story would always be her first priority, putting all of them in jeopardy. He hadn't listened. Now he was paying the price.

Stephanie had lost her career and her credibility as a sideline reporter for a major network when things had gone sideways three years before. Seemed she'd spent those years plotting her payback.

Nate picked up his beer and drained the bottle, then headed to the kitchen for another. The doorbell rang again.

He turned, his jaw clenched and his fist balled at his side.

All bets were off. Stephanie Weiss was about to get a piece of his mind—unfiltered. He'd just have to apologize to his mother later.

Kendra shifted her bag on her shoulder, her luggage at her side and her heart racing.

Nate wouldn't be happy to see her. Not when he'd dropped her at the hotel like she was a sack of flaming potatoes and pulled off, barely muttering two words.

When the door swung open, he looked angrier than she'd ever seen him. Like he was prepared for a fight. His shoulders drooped, a look of confusion on his face as he glanced around. "Kendra, what are you doing here?"

Nice to see you, too.

Kendra pulled her wrap around her to combat the chill in the air and the one rolling off her ex. "They were booked, except for a presidential suite. Same story with every other hotel I called. There are a couple of trade conventions in town this week."

"Forgot about that," he muttered, still blocking the doorway. He glanced over her shoulder again.

"If you're looking for your friend who just left, I passed her in the driveway."

"She isn't my friend. That was Stephanie Weiss."

"Your ex?" Kendra asked, then shifted under Nate's withering stare. "I mean, the reporter who started all of this?"

"Seems there are a lot of my exes showing up at my door tonight." He raised an eyebrow, then sighed. He grabbed her bags off the doorstep, opening the door wide enough for her to enter. "Come in."

Kendra stepped inside tentatively, glancing around the house. Despite the tension between them, she couldn't help smiling. She had so many great memories in this house. She remembered when Nate first bought the place. The weeks of house hunting before they'd finally settled on it. The times they'd shared there.

She glanced toward the den, where they'd last made love one weekend when she'd brought Kai to visit his father. They'd been in the middle of a heated argument about where Kai would spend Christmas. Then he'd kissed her, and they'd ended up making love on the sofa while their son slept blissfully unaware upstairs.

They'd almost made the same mistake in Montana.

Kendra stood taller. This time she'd be smarter. Stronger. Use better judgment. Then everything would be fine. "The place looks great."

"Thanks." Nate set her bags near the bottom of the stairs. "I'll take your bags up in a few minutes, but I was just about to get a beer. I could use one right now. Can I get you something?"

"Glass of wine?"

"Red or white?" he asked, then quickly answered his own question, echoing her response. "Rosé, of course."

She smiled. "If you have it. If not, a glass of white wine would be fine."

"Think I've got something in the cooler."

She followed him into the kitchen. "So, what was public enemy number one doing here?"

Nate's delts tensed visibly and he paused for a moment before reaching into the wine cooler. He dug through the bottles silently, then pulled out her favorite bottle of rosé. He opened the bottle. "Proposing a truce of sorts."

"So she acknowledges this is a vendetta against you?" Kendra sat at the kitchen table.

"Stephanie wanted me to know she was the one who took me down." He poured a glass of wine and handed it to Kendra. "She knows I can't do anything with the information."

Kendra thanked Nate for the rosé and took a sip. "Unfortunately, she's right. It would do more harm than good. You'll come off as a whiny athlete blaming someone else for your screwup."

Nate twisted the cap off his beer and sat at the table. He took a swig. "She's probably banking on me using that excuse at the press conference tomorrow. Bet she's already got a segment taped, just waiting for sound bites from the conference."

"Cunning, vindictive and determined. She's a real winner," Kendra muttered, then sipped her wine.

"Yeah, I can really pick 'em." He cut his gaze at her, then drank more of his beer.

Touché.

Kendra straightened her shoulders. "So this truce she offered, what was it?"

"She wanted me to give her an exclusive interview before the press conference. Said if I did, she wouldn't press the issue further."

"Indicating that if you don't, she'll keep fanning the flames." Kendra's stomach flipped. That meant she'd be doing more than just cleaning up the mess that was already made, she'd be putting out fires intentionally set by Stephanie. "Do you think she'd keep her word if you gave her the interview?"

"Not as far as I could throw her conniving ass."

Kendra nodded. "I suspected as much. If you don't mind my asking—"

"What did I see in her in the first place?" He finished her question. When she nodded, he continued, "I was out with an injury, feeling down on myself when I ran into Steph at the grocery store. I was struggling with my leg in a cast. She offered to help me shop and to make dinner for me that night. We were on friendly terms. Figured, what the hell? It could be fun."

"I'm sure it didn't hurt that she's very pretty. Wasn't she a beauty contestant or something?"

"Miss Connecticut. Third runner-up for Miss America that year." He didn't meet her gaze.

"Not judging." Kendra held her hands up. "But she obviously isn't as pretty on the inside."

Nate grunted. "Got that right."

"Okay, so taking the deal isn't an option. We'll have to be prepared for whatever she slings our way."

Kendra paused before asking the thing she needed to know, but didn't want to ask. "She doesn't have anything on you, does she? No secretly recorded audio, no sex tapes?"

"No," he said emphatically, sitting up straight as a rod, then dropping his gaze. "I mean, not that I'm aware of."

Fair enough. Anyone could set up a secret camera in their bedroom.

"Anything you might have told her about a teammate or your family that she might use?"

"Not that I recall." His response wasn't as convincing. "Like I said, we were only together a few months. The time we did spend together…we spent very little of it talking."

Kendra ignored the twisting in her gut. "Then we'll just stay alert. Be sure not to give her any new ammunition."

Nate stood suddenly. "Got a long day tomorrow. I'll take your bags to your room."

He was gone before she could thank him.

Kendra poured herself another glass of wine. This time she'd be ready for Stephanie Weiss.

Chapter 11

Nate took his place behind the lectern and straightened his tie. He adjusted the microphone and thanked everyone for coming, then explained that he would play the full video.

Stephanie pressed her lips into an angry slash and folded her arms. Her ire confirmed that playing the entire video was the right move.

Score one more for Kendra.

He stepped aside while the five-minute video played in its entirety. Nate glanced over at Marcus and Kendra standing in the corner.

His brother nodded reassuringly. Kendra's confident smile filled his chest with warmth and eased the tension in his shoulders. He wouldn't admit it to Marcus, but he was glad Kendra was there. Especially since his twin sister—off on one of the solo island vacations she took a few times a year—couldn't be.

When the video ended, the lights came on again. Nate launched into a prepared script, giving a brief overview of what happened that night and why he was so frustrated with himself and his teammates. He made it clear he'd offered his sincere apologies in person to everyone who was available. Nate apologized again for his lack of thoughtfulness and the impact it had on his teammates and the Marauders organization.

He ended by stating emphatically that he intended to suit up for the Marauders for the remainder of his career.

"Our team has come so close to going to the big dance. During the off-season, we'll work hard as individuals and as an organization to ensure we're giving our all every single time we take the field. It's what every man on the team wants. Most important, it's what the loyal fans of this city deserve. Thank you for coming."

Nate stepped away from the microphone, relieved the press conference was finally over. He was especially grateful Kendra insisted they not take questions.

Score two for Kendra.

"Is it true you just returned from Montana where you pressured Wade Willis to retire before next season?" Stephanie shot to her feet, to the surprise of everyone in the room.

"Of course not." The words came out of his mouth before he could stop them. Kendra had already warned him someone was bound to push for questions. He was supposed to say, "No further comment."

So much for that.

"Wade is still one of the elite quarterbacks in this

league. This past year wasn't his best year, but it wasn't mine, either. We'll both be stronger next year."

"So you admit you're a big part of the reason the team has stalled in the play-offs three years in a row?" Stephanie could barely hold back her smirk.

Nate's shoulders knotted. He pressed his lips into a harsh line and breathed out slowly. "As I stated that night on the video, I need to be better. We all do. No further questions."

He stepped away from the microphone and made a beeline behind the curtains and away from the hungry pack of jackals clamoring to ask the next question. Nate pressed his back against the wall, angry with himself for not sticking to the script. He'd let Stephanie rile him. She knew he wouldn't let that accusation hang in the air, unanswered.

And how the hell did she know he'd just returned from Montana, anyway?

He looked up at the *click* of Kendra's heels coming down the hallway. She wasn't happy. Neither was Marcus, who was hard on her heels.

"Why didn't you stick to the script?" Marcus gestured wildly. "Were we not clear about not taking questions?"

"I know I should've ignored her question, but I couldn't leave the fans thinking I'm trying to push Wade out."

"There are going to be a lot of accusations hurled at you in the next few weeks, man. You can't respond to every one. We've got a plan. If you stick with it, everything will be fine." Marcus stormed away, likely in search of a strong cup of coffee.

Nate turned his attention to Kendra. "Go ahead. Let me have it."

Kendra's expression softened, and she let out a quiet sigh as she squeezed his arm. "I know how much Wade means to you and to the fans. It's probably good you combated that accusation right away and that you spoke so highly of him. You handled the situation well."

"Really?"

"Really. Just don't do it again. If we say no questions, then don't address questions. Not even from Stephanie Weiss. Got it?"

"Got it." He looked down at his watch. "We better head out. Marcus and I have a late lunch meeting over at the foundation. We'll drop you off at the house on the way."

"Aren't we flying back to Pleasure Cove tonight?" Her shoulders tensed and there was a hint of panic in the slight elevation of her tone.

"Change of plans. I finally connected with Dade. We're meeting tomorrow for lunch, so we'll have to stay one more night. Hope that's cool."

"It's important that you sit down with Dade and iron things out." Kendra waved a hand. "I'll try again with the hotels."

"No need." Nate shoved his hands in his pockets. "There's plenty of room for both of us."

"If you're sure."

"I am. Feel free to work from my office. I'll even make dinner tonight. To thank you for everything," he added quickly.

She cocked an eyebrow, her adorable nose crinkling. "You cook now?"

"Okay, so maybe I'm just heating it up. Same difference."

Kendra laughed, then looked thoughtful, the gears turning in that brilliant head of hers. She nodded reluctantly. "Sure."

He gave her a quick nod, then they headed toward the exit, his heart dancing with a growing sense of hope.

Kendra paced in front of the fireplace in the den, her body filled with nervous energy, prompted by the memories of when she was last there.

She halted, catching her breath as she fought back the vivid sensation of Nate planting soft kisses along her collarbone and shoulders. Kisses that led to a wild and passionate night together.

Kendra swallowed hard, then resumed her pacing. Finally, she plopped on the sofa and pulled out her phone. She called her mother, but there was no answer. Next, she called her sister.

"How's the trip?"

Kendra released a slow breath, fortified by the lilt in Maya's voice. "Professionally? Things are going well. Personally? I'm losing it."

"Why, what's going on between you and Nate?"

"I'm sitting on the infamous sofa, trying my hardest to keep my head together, but all I keep thinking about is the last time I was here, when I couldn't keep my legs together."

Maya chuckled. "What are you doing at Nate's anyway? Thought you were staying at a hotel."

"So did I, but we ended up staying overnight in Montana sharing Wade and Greer's guesthouse."

Maya cleared her throat. "The more important question is, did you two share a bed?"

"No," Kendra said quickly. The silence seemed to extend forever. Her sister was the master of the well-used pause to get her to spill her guts. She groaned. "But he kissed me."

"Did you kiss him back?" The lilt returned to Maya's voice. She was on the verge of a giggle.

"Until I regained my clarity."

"Clarity, huh? Sounds more like delusion, if you're still pretending Nate doesn't mean anything to you."

"Of course he does. He's Kai's dad. He was my best friend. My first." She said the words wistfully, recalling that weekend her mother had taken her brother to Raleigh on a college tour. "I'll always care for him. That doesn't mean we're meant to be together."

"And what does Nate think?" Maya's tone was subdued.

Kendra swung her legs beneath her and exhaled. "He wants us to be a family."

"Oh my gosh, Kendra. That's great news." Maya paused when Kendra didn't respond. "Isn't it?"

"Seems like it's more about Nate wanting to be with Kai." A dull ache filled her chest. "He didn't say he wanted to be with me. He just keeps going on about how great it would be to finally be a family."

"Nate loves his son. Why is that bad?"

"Because it can't be the only reason we're together, like it was for Dad when he married my mom."

There was an uneasy silence between them. As much as Kendra loved Maya now, it hadn't always been that way. Kendra had resented Maya and her younger brother.

She couldn't shake the hurt of knowing she was the reason her father left. Curtis Williams abandoned their family less than a year after her birth.

Though he'd left them behind, he chose to stay with Maya's mother just a year later. They'd gotten married and raised two kids. He'd attended every school function and proudly filmed everything from Maya's and Cole's first steps to their college graduations.

Even now, she sometimes lay awake at night wondering why her father hadn't loved her enough to stay with them. Why he hadn't doted on her and Dash and embraced being their dad as much as he enjoyed being a father to Maya and Cole.

"I don't think it's as simple as that." Maya adored Curtis Williams. She was a daddy's girl. He'd been there for her all her life. Why shouldn't she adore him? "He loved your mom."

Kendra snorted. "He had a damn funny way of showing it. Love like that, I don't need."

"Nate isn't our dad," Maya said quietly. "And for the record, Dad was young and he made his mistakes. He regrets how poorly he handled things."

"Agree to disagree." It was Kendra's signal for Maya to end the discussion of Curtis Williams's virtues.

"Okay." The word came out of Maya's mouth in an odd singsong. "But you're not being fair to Nate. Just because being a family is important to him doesn't mean you aren't."

Kendra understood the sense of indebtedness Maya felt toward Nate. She and Dash had wanted nothing to do with their father or their half siblings. Still, Maya had been persistent, following Kendra to college. Nate and his parents encouraged her to get to know Maya.

"She's family," Nate's mom, Ms. Naomi, had said. "Doesn't matter how she became family. She just is. And you don't turn your back on family."

Kendra had resented Nate's interference at first, but she and Dash had grown apart as they'd gotten older and she yearned for the deep connection Nate had with his siblings.

Getting to know and accept her younger sister was one of the best decisions she'd ever made. She and Maya owed a huge debt of gratitude to the Johnstons. But she wouldn't be with Nate out of a sense of obligation.

"We're not the same people we were seven years ago." Kendra stood by the fireplace, allowing its warmth to soothe the chill creeping down her spine.

"So get to know each other again. Most important, tell him how you feel," Maya urged.

Kendra's temples throbbed. "I can't."

"Why not?"

"He'll say it just because I need to hear it." Kendra paced in front of the fireplace. Her slippers scuffed against the carpet.

"Nate always says what he feels. That's why he's in the spot he's in now." Maya sighed in response to the cluck of Kendra's tongue. "If he says it, it's because he means it."

"Then why didn't he say it the other night? Why didn't he say he misses me? That he wants to be with me? That he can't stop thinking of me the way I can't stop thinking of him?" Kendra hadn't meant to say the last part, but her mouth was moving faster than her brain.

Maya hesitated before she responded. "The last time

Nate confessed his feelings for you, you rejected him and walked away. Can you blame him for being gun-shy?"

Kendra's stomach twisted in knots as the truth of Maya's words hit her squarely in the chest. She didn't respond.

"Maybe Nate's reluctant to share his feelings because he isn't sure he can trust you with them." An apologetic tone filtered her sister's brutally honest words.

"Maybe. Still, I won't get back with Nate for the wrong reasons. As much as I know Kai wants his dad and me to be together, it would be worse if things blew up a few years down the road. I won't set him up for the disappointment and resentment I experienced at his age."

"You mean, the resentment you feel now." Maya's voice wavered.

"I don't mean to make you feel bad. That's why I try not to talk about Dad. It's never a conversation that will go well between us."

"Even when we don't discuss him, that ugly little truth is hidden in the words we don't say." Maya cleared her throat. "Do you have any idea how much it hurts to know that deep down my sister wishes I were never born?"

"That isn't true."

"I wish it were as easy for me to believe that as it is for you." Maya sighed. "If it were the other way around, maybe I'd feel the same."

"No, you wouldn't. You're the sweetest, most loving person I know. I know it doesn't always seem like it, but I'm grateful to have you in my life. I'm thrilled you found someone who loves you as much as I do. You deserve a great guy like Liam. He's about as close as a guy can get to being worthy of you."

"Thanks, sis." The smile returned to Maya's voice.

"Speaking of that handsome man of yours, when are you two going to finally set a date?" Kendra settled onto the couch.

"I was thinking we'd wait until next summer to get married."

"Why so long? Is it a family thing for him?" The Westbrooks owned a huge international resort firm based in London, and they were well connected back in the UK.

"It's nothing like that, it's just... I keep hoping that if I wait long enough, you and Dad will work things out."

"I promised I'd be on my best behavior on your wedding day," Kendra reminded her sister.

"I appreciate the sentiment, but the reality is that the tension between you two makes everyone uncomfortable."

"I won't let that happen on your wedding day, Maya. I promise."

"The minute you see him, you'll pick a fight. Happens every time." Maya's voice rose to a crescendo. Suddenly it became sad. "You're not just punishing Dad. It hurts that I can't sit down with two of my favorite people on my wedding day."

Kendra's heart ached. Whatever her issues were with their father, Maya wasn't to blame. "I'm sorry. I had no idea."

"I know, but we can talk about that another day. Right now, let's talk about the real reason you called. You're still in love with Nate, and it terrifies you."

Kendra didn't deny the accusation. "I won't break his heart again. He couldn't take that. Neither could I. Besides, his evil twin would probably strangle me with her bare hands."

"Or at least hire someone to off you." Maya laughed, the tension between them easing.

"No, she'd definitely do it herself." Kendra was only half kidding. Vi would probably relish the feel of her warm blood on her hands. Nate's twin could be your best friend or your worst enemy. Once the former, Kendra was now the latter.

"The solution is simple," Maya said. "Don't break his heart this time."

That was Maya. Making a complicated relationship like the one she and Nate shared seem so simple. Apparently, she'd forgotten what a convoluted relationship she and Liam had just a few months prior. When she was still terrified of bringing someone new into her daughters' lives, afraid Liam would disappoint them.

Thankfully, she'd been wrong. Liam was an amazing man who'd left behind his playboy ways once he found the woman of his dreams—her little sister.

"I didn't set out to break his heart before. I panicked. How can I be sure it won't happen again?"

"You can't, but you can be honest with Nate and yourself about what freaked you out then." Maya's voice was soothing. "And any lingering fears holding you back now."

"I won't put my career aside for Nate again," Kendra suddenly interjected. The declaration took her by surprise.

"Then talk to him," Maya said simply. "No more excuses."

She was gone before Kendra could object.

"They're not excuses," she said to the empty room as she tossed her phone on the sofa. "It's the truth."

"What's the truth?"

Kendra startled, nearly jumping out of her skin. "Nate, I didn't hear you come in."

He grinned. "Obviously. You hungry?"

Kendra nodded. Until he'd mentioned it, she hadn't realized how hungry she was. She'd checked the fridge earlier, but there was very little edible food left. "I could eat."

A slow grin stretched his mouth. "Good, because I thought we could cook together like the old days."

Damn. Now she couldn't look at the kitchen counter without reminiscing about exactly how those times nearly always ended.

Who knew kitchen sex could be so good?

Kendra shrugged. "Okay."

She would help Nate cook because she was hungry. Starving, in fact. But no matter what, they most definitely would not go there. No matter how good he looked in that slim gray suit.

Chapter 12

One of the many things Nate missed about Kendra was their shared love of food. She'd never subsisted on lettuce or gone from one crazy fad diet to the next.

Kendra appreciated a gourmet meal. Savored every bite. Watching her enjoy a perfectly cooked steak or authentic pasta dish was practically foreplay.

Tonight, he would begin his slow seduction by making her favorite meal. He'd nixed his plans to purchase a premade lasagna prepared by a local gourmet chef. Kendra's crack about his not being able to cook forced him to step up his game.

He purchased the meal plan that came with the ingredients and the recipe so they could prepare the meal together, like they did when they first started out.

Nate's pulse quickened as he reminisced over those steamy nights together. There was something almost erotic about the act of cooking together. Filling one basic need led to satisfying another.

He set the bags on the counter and took off his jacket, folding it across the chair. "Can I get you a drink?"

Her hesitant nod, a brief glimpse at the vulnerability she loathed revealing, somehow made her even sexier. "Half a glass of wine would be great."

Nate dragged his gaze up her body, admiring her toned curves. She wore an oversize white T-shirt with a deep vee over a pair of black leggings that hugged her ample hips and thighs. He cleared his throat, raising his eyes to hers again as he pulled a chilled bottle of her favorite rosé from the bag. He poured her a half glass and watched her sensual mouth as she took a generous sip, her hand unsteady.

"Everything okay?" Nate removed one cuff link, then the other.

"Fine." Her voice vibrated with false bravado.

He excused himself to change. When he returned in jeans and a T-shirt, Kendra had removed the lasagna ingredients from the bag and lined them up on the counter. A pot of water was boiling on the stove.

"I think you've forgotten how this whole 'cooking together' thing works."

Kendra snorted. "All I did was unpack the bag. There's plenty left to do."

He washed and dried his hands, then opened the package of pasta noodles, adding them to the salted water. He set the timer, then took out a large skillet and placed it on the burner.

Kendra peeled and sliced an onion while Nate added Italian sausage and ground beef to the pan.

They worked together in comfortable silence. Nate had missed this. He hadn't realized what a luxury it was to be with someone he was so in tune with that he felt the comfort of her presence without either of them uttering a single word.

Kendra was the only woman with whom he'd felt that kind of warmth and security.

"There." Kendra added the onions and garlic to the skillet as he browned its contents.

"Thank you." He forced the words past the thickness in his throat. It was something he wanted to say since that moment at Wade's when she'd placed her hand on his, calming him when it felt like his world was spinning out of control.

"For helping to make my dinner?" Kendra rummaged through the drawers and retrieved the can opener. He'd upgraded the utensil, but kept it in the same place she'd designated for it when they were together. In fact, the entire kitchen was essentially just as she'd arranged it. Like it was stuck in time. "It's the least I can do."

Nate reduced the flame, then turned to face her, taking her soft, warm hand in his. He pulled her closer and she leaned in to him, her eyes meeting his.

"For taking me on as a client, even though I didn't want to work with you initially. For coming with me on this trip. For being the voice of reason when I needed it most."

She didn't speak. Instead she leaned in closer, meeting him halfway as he captured her warm mouth in a kiss. He slipped his fingers in her hair, his tongue tangling with hers.

Kendra wrapped her arms around him and lifted

onto her toes, as if trying to capture more of his mouth. One hand trailed down her back and over her backside.

He missed the feel of her body, pressed against his, and the taste of her sweet mouth. The way her body fit perfectly against his. The elevation of his temperature and the rapid beat of his heart whenever she was in his arms.

How could she not miss this?

Nate gripped her bottom, pulling her tightly against him, enjoying the feel of their bodies pressed together.

He swallowed the soft gasp that escaped her throat in response. She dropped the can opener. The sound of it crashing against the hard tile floor startled them both.

Kendra pulled away. She retrieved the utensil and returned to the work of opening the cans, her eyes focused on her task. "Thank you for saying that, but hold your gratitude until I get the results you're looking for. Because I will."

"I don't doubt that." Nate sighed and went back to stirring the contents of the skillet. Bits of garlic and onion had burned. "But regardless of what happens, I want you to know I'm grateful for what you've done. I appreciate you. I didn't say that enough when we were together. It's a mistake I won't repeat."

"Thank you for giving me this shot." Kendra's eyes met his. "Most exes wouldn't be so gracious."

Nate's heart sank in his chest. He resented the fact that their romantic relationship was firmly in the past. A harsh reality that made his chest ache. Kendra seemed content with it. Able to turn her feelings on and off at will.

The hunger that consumed him wasn't reflected in

Kendra's eyes. There was desire, but not the abject need that arose whenever he thought of her. Certainly not with the ferocity with which he felt it. If she'd felt that strongly about him, she would've jumped at his proposal to try again.

Despite the bulletproof force field she projected, Nate was sure her true feelings were buried below the surface, where she could keep them safe.

Even if she refused to acknowledge her feelings, Nate knew Kendra still loved him. It was evidenced by a thousand little things. The affectionate tone of her voice, the dreamy gaze when their eyes met and the soothing touch of her hand. It was couched in all the words she couldn't say.

This time, though, he needed to be sure before he poured out his heart to her.

He loved Kendra, but he wouldn't make a fool of himself again. He couldn't endure the pain and humiliation of another rejection. The feeling of his heart being pierced by jagged, broken glass.

This time, he needed to hear her say the words first. That she loved him and needed him in her life. That she wanted to be with him.

"You're not just an ex." He loosened bits of browned sausage and garlic stuck to the bottom of the pan. "We have a son together, and we were best friends for most of our lives."

A sad smile barely lifted the corner of her mouth as she scraped tomato paste from a can with a small rubber spatula. "That's why we're such good co-parents. Maybe we aren't exactly friends now, but we have that foundation to rely on."

Now it was his turn to snort.

"What did I say wrong?" She set down the empty can, then started to empty the next into the skillet.

"*Co-parents*. That term is a joke. It implies both parties are equal parents, but that's not really possible, is it? One person is always left on the outside, looking in. Wishing they were there in those photos. In the moments that matter. The ones you'll never get back."

Kendra looked thoughtful as she opened one can of tomato sauce, then the other. She poured both into the pan, then carried all of the empty cans over to the sink and rinsed them before tossing them into the recycle bin.

"This isn't how I envisioned my life, either, but it's the best option we have." Her tone was faint, apologetic. She wiped her hands on a towel. "Things could be a lot worse. Every day, I'm thankful Kai has you in his life."

"And every night I go to bed regretting that I can't be in his life every day, the way my dad has always been in mine." Hurt and anger rose in his chest. When he met her gaze, her eyes were filled with tears. "Kendra, I'm sorry. I didn't mean to—"

"I can't do this and still do my job, Nate." She cut him off, shaking her head. "Right now, doing my job is more important." She turned to leave.

When would he learn to keep his big mouth shut?

"I didn't mean to upset you." Nate sighed, catching her elbow. "Would I be making you a home-cooked meal right now if I intended to say something stupid and ruin our night?"

"What you said wasn't stupid. You're right. I made a bad decision, but you're the one who's had to suffer most. It isn't fair. So I promise, after this is all over, we'll work out a more fair arrangement so you get to spend more time with Kai."

"You'd do that?" Nate was stunned. Kai meant everything to her. "You'd be willing to sacrifice some of your time with him?"

She nodded, her lips pursed and her eyes glossy.

"That means a lot to me." He cleared his throat. "But being together as a family would mean even more."

"As much as we love Kai, we can't be together just for his sake. Neither of us would be happy. I want more than that for myself and for you."

"Shouldn't I get to decide what's best for me?"

"I'm sorry." Kendra pulled free from him, her cheeks suddenly wet with tears. "Excuse me."

She rushed from the room and up the stairs.

Dammit.

He'd blown it again.

Nate finished up the lasagna sauce by adding the supplied herbs and seasonings. Then he let it simmer while he drained the noodles. A half hour had passed and Kendra hadn't returned.

His pride hadn't allowed him to go after her following the proposal debacle seven years ago. He wouldn't make that mistake again. If she wasn't back by the time the sauce finished simmering, he'd go and find her.

Kendra cupped her hands under the cold running water in Nate's guest bathroom and splashed it on her face. Her eyes were red, her cheeks were stained with tears and her mascara was a runny mess. Better to strip it all off than to attempt to fix it.

She removed her makeup, cleansed her skin, then patted her face dry with a towel.

Standing there, her face stripped of all makeup, she felt nearly as vulnerable as she had when Nate told her what he thought of her co-parenting.

She'd been lying to herself. Pretending things were good for all of them, when the truth was they were all miserable.

Kai missed being with his dad. Nate was hurting without his son. She lived with the guilt of being the coward who broke up their family because she couldn't deal with her daddy issues.

"Thanks, Dad," she groaned. "You produced one damaged little girl."

There was a tap at the bathroom door. "Kendra, are you okay?"

She opened the door partially. "I didn't expect to take so long. I'll be down in a sec."

"You've been crying." Nate reached his long arm through the door and cradled her cheek in his large palm. "I didn't intend to upset you."

Loosening her grip on the door handle, Kendra leaned into his palm, her eyes drifting shut. She savored his touch—strong, yet delicate—and the warmth of his rough palm against her cool cheek. Heat radiated into her neck and down her spine. A soothing lightness seeped into her bones, and a sense of calm settled over her.

Her eyes fluttered open. Something in Nate's brown eyes was so tender and sweet it melted her heart. Yet the heat in his penetrating gaze and feather-soft touch took her breath away.

She inhaled, dropping her gaze to his stubbled chin. "Nate, I'm sorry I—"

Nate pressed his open mouth to hers, cradling the back of her neck.

Kendra didn't object to his kiss or the way he slung an arm low around her waist, pulling their bodies together, his firm erection pressed to her belly.

A soft gasp escaped her mouth as his tongue moved against hers. Her fingertips glided up the soft cotton of his shirt. She pressed them to his back through the fabric, aching to touch his heated skin.

Each soft kiss Nate planted along her jawline and down her throat ignited flames along her skin.

"I want you, Dray. Here. Now. Tell me you want me, too," he murmured between kisses.

Her hot, liquid center melted a little more at hearing him use his pet name for her. He hadn't done that since the day she walked out of his life. Not even those nights in Memphis.

"I do." No point in denying the obvious. Her beaded nipples pressed into his chest and her breath came in shallow pants. "But if we do this, you have to understand—"

The muscles of his back stiffened as his eyes met hers. "That it doesn't mean anything?"

She stroked his cheek. "Being with you could never not mean anything to me. But it isn't a promise or a commitment. It's just sex."

He frowned, lines spanning his forehead.

"I want this, I do." She placed a soft hand on his stern jaw, and his eyes met hers again. "But you mean so much to me. My relationship with you is more important than this."

He didn't respond right away. For a moment, Kendra expected him to release her and walk away. Instead, he pressed his mouth to hers and kissed her again. His tongue tangled with hers as he gripped her bottom, pulling her hard against him.

Kendra moaned against his lips, giving in to the prickle of electricity dancing along her spine, igniting low in her belly.

Nate surprised her, scooping her into his arms and carrying her down the hall toward his large master bedroom. He nudged open the double doors with his foot, then laid her on his bed.

Kendra looked around the room. The kitchen had been essentially the same, but this room looked completely different. He'd made a concerted effort to erase any trace of her.

She had no right to be hurt. Yet she was. The walls were a dove gray now, instead of the cocoa beige they'd selected together when he bought the place.

The bed and all the other furniture were different, too. Large, sleek ebony wood pieces. Dark and masculine. All hard lines. None of the soft, organic curves she preferred.

Nate brought her back from her disquieting thoughts with a kiss. His hand trailed down her side, gripping her thigh as he settled between her legs. She whimpered at the sensation of his length pressed to the juncture of her thighs. Her breath became shallow as the heat and electricity building there spread throughout her body. Made her feel like she was floating in a pool of warm water, the steam so intense she could barely breathe.

Nate pulled his mouth from hers, their eyes meeting as he took her in. Something in that dark gaze made her feel as if there were nothing in the world he wanted more than her. And damn if that stare didn't multiply his raw sex appeal by a factor of ten.

Nate planted feverish kisses on her throat that trailed down the vee of her shirt. She inhaled the coconut scent wafting from his dark curls and tried to get out of her own head and enjoy it.

Breathe. Just breathe.

"Stop trying to talk yourself out of this." Nate's husky whisper brought her attention back to him, away from the battle raging between her body and her mind. "There's nothing wrong with two people who care for each other as much as we do being together. Even if one of them believes it's just sex."

"Nate, you promised—"

"Relax, Dray. I know where we stand." There was a hint of strain in his voice and in the tension between his brows. "We're cool, no matter what happens tonight."

She breathed a little easier. "Then what are you still doing in that shirt?"

Nate traced her mouth with his thumb, then kissed her again. "Good question. I could ask you the same."

She gripped the hem of his shirt and tugged it up. He adjusted, allowing her to remove the garment. Next, she shed hers. Kendra pressed her fingers to his back as she pulled him to her again. "Much better."

"A little better." He glided his large palm down her hip and thigh, his eyes locked on hers. "You naked would be a hell of a lot better."

"I can make that happen." She lifted her hips, allowing him to slide off her panties and leggings. Her bra and his jeans soon followed.

"Hey." Kendra snapped the waistband of his underwear. "You're not completely undressed."

"Gotta keep my focus, babe," Nate responded between nibbles and kisses that trailed between her breasts. "Make this last."

Can't argue with that philosophy.

"Fine for now, but—" She inhaled sharply when Nate caressed a stiff peak with his firm tongue. The sensation traveled straight to her sex. "Not fair."

Nate chuckled, the sound vibrating in her chest. He kissed his way across the valley between her breasts and swirled his tongue around her other nipple, causing a rush of dampness at her core. "Who said anything about this being fair?" He trailed kisses down her belly. Each one caused her breath to come quicker as he approached the space between her thighs. "I plan to use every trick in the book to make you reconsider."

A shiver ran down her spine as he lapped at her hardened nub. She gripped the bedding and dug her heels into the mattress. "Nate, that feels incredible."

She'd nearly forgotten how deft Nate Johnston was with that tongue. He hadn't gone there the last two times they were together. Those incidents involved quick, hot, angry sex. This was slow and deliberate.

He wrapped his arms around her thighs, pinning her in place as his tongue grazed her clit and the swollen, engorged flesh surrounding it.

The higher she sailed, the quicker his movements. She was trembling, cursing. Almost there. Suddenly he slowed things down with deliberate laps of his tongue, heightening the sensation.

Kendra's breathing slowed, though her heart still beat a mile a minute. She tangled her fingers in his hair as he worshipped her sex, bringing her to the edge again.

A jolt of desire ran through her veins as Nate plunged his tongue inside her, then slowly withdrew it. She moaned softly, her tense muscles quivering in response to the delicious rhythm. Kendra whimpered, calling his name and begging him not to stop, as she dug her heels into the mattress and clutched the back of his head.

His sly grin indicated he had no intention of stopping until he'd brought her over the edge.

And he did.

The orgasm hit her, hard and sudden. Her legs trembled and her belly contracted. She shut her eyes, allowing the intense feeling of satisfaction to wash over her like warm, soothing water.

Nate trailed kisses over her mound, up her stomach and between her breasts. He gently bit and sucked her neck, as if marking his territory like he did when they were in high school.

He pressed his lips to her ear. "This body will always be mine. No matter where you go or what you do."

His claim was even more arousing than what he'd just done to her body. She wanted to contradict him. Make it clear that her body belonged to her and no one else. But she understood what he meant. *No one will ever make you feel this way. Have you crawling out of your skin, calling his name.*

If the past seven years were any indication, he was right. She'd been with a handful of guys in the time they'd been apart. She could sum up the collective experience with one word.

Disappointing.

Nate never disappointed her. He sent her soaring,

shaking, calling his name. Their bodies fit together as if they were designed for each other.

As she stared into his handsome face, hovering over hers, she couldn't deny his claim.

Her body did belong to Nate Johnston, as did her heart.

Chapter 13

Nate kissed the side of Kendra's face, glistening with sweat. It was the middle of winter, but suddenly his sprawling bedroom felt intimate, the space sultry.

Kendra's chest rose and fell as she tried to catch her breath. She hadn't responded to his declaration that her body belonged to him, but had she disagreed, she would've told him so in no uncertain terms. Kendra's silence indicated her reluctant concession to the truth of his words.

We belong together.

They would be again soon, if it was up to him.

"I love watching you come apart like that. It's still the sexiest thing I've ever seen." He kissed her neck and trailed a finger down the center of her chest. "You will always be the most beautiful woman in the world to me."

Kendra's eyes twinkled as she swiped a finger beneath them. A wide smile spread across her face.

Nate kissed her again, then crawled off the bed and dug into his bedside table and sheathed himself. He joined Kendra beneath the covers and kissed her neck, her shoulders.

He'd tried hating her for breaking his heart. He'd tried to replace her with women who were beautiful or famous. None of them made him feel the way he did when he was with her.

It was Kendra he wanted in his bed and in his life. The woman who owned his heart and bore his son. The woman he wanted to retire to Pleasure Cove with and have more children.

The words he wanted to say stuck at the back of his throat. *I love you. I need you. Please, come back.* Instead, he kissed her fervently, conveying everything he felt through his kiss, his touch.

He glided his hands along her warm, slick skin. Caressed her back. Squeezed her hips and the swell of her breasts. Laved her tight, beaded tips with his hungry tongue. He coaxed her back to the edge of the precipice, her body responding to every touch, every kiss.

"Nate, I need you." Kendra's breathy plea nearly broke him down. She gripped his ass, bringing him closer. Increasing the friction of his sheathed length grazing her slick bud. "Please."

His plans to continue teasing her, making her want him more, flew out the window the moment he gazed into those seductive brown eyes. They drained every ounce of his willpower. If she asked right now, he'd give her anything.

He pumped his thick shaft, his body already aching with desire for her. She whimpered quietly as he slid inside her, taking his time. He savored the slow, painstaking reintroduction to every damn inch of her.

He groaned, pressed his lips together as his eyes drifted closed at the sensation of being surrounded by her warm, slick flesh. Nate tried to hold it together as he slowly moved his hips, delighting in every hiss, every whimper coming from her sweet lips.

Nate cursed, his brow damp with sweat. She felt so damn good. Better than he remembered. Her delicate scent mingled with the smell of sweat and sex.

He wanted her in his bed. Every. Single. Night. He would remind her how good they'd been together. How good they could be again.

Nate leaned his weight forward, grinding against her as he entered her. He increased the friction against her hardened nub. Watched the parting of her lips until finally she cried out, writhing and calling his name.

His shoulders relaxed even as he continued his movement, heightening her pleasure until he reached his release. Muscles tense and heart racing, Nate dropped onto the mattress beside her. He tugged the covers over them as he caught his breath.

"I know we shouldn't have done that," she said, finally, one hand pressed to his chest, "but it was incredible."

"Who says we shouldn't?" He chafed at the implication that what they'd done was wrong. "We don't have to answer to anyone."

Kendra frowned, raising her head. "Was that the doorbell?"

Nate strained to listen, but didn't hear anything. "I don't think so."

The bell rang again. This time he heard it.

"See. There it goes again." Panic rose on Kendra's face as she pulled the covers up higher.

"Whoever it is, they'll go away." Nate wrapped an arm around her. As long as it had taken him to get her to bed, he had no plans of letting anything interrupt the moment.

Kendra settled against his chest. She was silent. Pensive.

Nate massaged her back, trying to relax Kendra and return to the blissful afterglow they enjoyed a moment before. A space where it was only the two of them and nothing else mattered. That's where they needed to be if he was going to convince her to stop running from her feelings for him.

He picked up the remote and turned on a streaming audio service, hoping the soft vocals of Luther Vandross and Anita Baker would soothe her.

She propped her chin on his chest. "What if it's important?"

"They'll come back." He kissed her forehead. "Besides, if it were that important, they would've called first."

"I did call first, lover boy, but you left your phone downstairs."

Kendra scrambled to pull the covers up to her chin, and Nate held the sheet firmly in place so she wouldn't uncover all his business to his nosy-ass twin sister.

"For real, Vi? I did not give you the key to my place so you could stroll up in here whenever you please. It's for emergencies."

"Seems like an emergency to me." Vi folded her arms and leaned against the doorjamb. "'Cause I'm pretty sure you've lost your natural mind. I go on vacation for two weeks and all hell breaks loose. Your face is all over the news and now she's all up in your business and in your bed."

Nate clenched his teeth. "Look, Vi, I know you're just trying to look out for me, but you are completely out of line. Now that you're back we can talk about your concerns, but at a more appropriate time. Like tomorrow morning."

Vi gave Kendra her evil stare before returning her attention to Nate. "We need to talk now. Before things get worse."

"I messed up with that video, but I do not need you to babysit me."

"So you don't trust me to look after you, but you and Marcus think it's a good idea to trust her?" Vi pointed at Kendra accusingly.

"That's my choice. Just like it was my choice to have you run the foundation, even though half our family didn't think you were levelheaded enough to handle a responsibility like that."

"So now you're going to throw me under the bus because I'm pointing out the obvious. Ms. Thing here doesn't have your back. She never did."

"That's enough!" Nate blared, his chest heaving and heat crawling up his neck. "I get that you're angry, but don't take it out on Kendra. I made the choice to work with her. Beyond that, she's my son's mother. So you will never, *ever* talk to her like that again. Got it?"

Vi rolled her eyes, then shrugged.

"I mean it." He pointed a finger at his sister.

"Fine. Okay. Sorry." She threw her hands up. "But

we do need to talk. Now. Meet you downstairs in ten." Navia left, slamming the bedroom door behind her.

Nate pressed his palms to his eye sockets and shook his head. "Sorry about that. Vi's been out of the country, so we haven't had a chance to talk about this. She'll be fine. I just need to make it clear that this isn't her choice."

"She hates me." Kendra tucked a few curls behind her ear. "You guys are incredibly close. She feels your pain, maybe more intensely."

"Is that why you didn't say a word when she was in here clowning?" When she shrugged, Nate cupped her chin. "That isn't the fierce warrior I know. If we're going to work together, you'll have to deal with Vi. Don't let her run you over. You never did before. You know Vi, if you give her an inch she'll take the length of two football fields before you can blink. I'll set her straight, but promise me you won't take any shit from her."

"We'll work it out." Kendra's tone was less than convincing, but he let it go.

Nate slipped his fingers into her hair, pulling her closer. He kissed her. "Don't move. I'll be back with dinner." He winked.

Kendra slapped a hand over her mouth. "Dinner! God, I hope it isn't ruined."

"It isn't. It's fine." Nate got out of bed, retrieved his clothing from the floor and dressed. "Sit tight. I'll be back as soon as I get rid of Vi." He leaned in and kissed her forehead. "Promise."

"Don't be so hard on her, Nate. She's just trying to protect you. It's been her job since you two were conceived." She smiled, but then her expression and tone grew serious. "I won't come between you two. I'd rather walk away."

"I know you would." He gripped the door handle. "Fortunately, it won't come to that. Working with you is exactly what I need right now. We've already made progress. Bottom line? If she really wants what's best for me, she'll get on board. She'll complain about how rough the ride is, but she'll come aboard just the same."

Nate closed the bedroom door, then padded down the stairs in his bare feet to straighten out his nosy, overprotective, older-by-five-minutes twin sister.

His sister had the worst timing. He'd finally made headway with Kendra, and Vi decided to return from her vacation two days early. He stepped into the kitchen, where his sister paced the floor.

"What the hell is she doing here?" That was Vi. She didn't waste a moment, just got right into it.

Nate gritted his teeth and counted to ten as he rummaged in the freezer for one of the beers Kendra put on ice. "You're not my wife or my mother. So why do you care?"

Vi snorted in the unladylike manner that signaled a smart-ass comment was on the horizon. With one hand on her hip, she shoved a finger in his direction. "If you stopped thinking with the head below your belt and started using the one above your shoulders, I wouldn't need to act like your mama."

Maybe she has me there.

He'd never admit that to her. Vi already thought she knew better than everyone in their family when it came to their careers, love lives and how they raised their kids. Never mind that she had zero expertise with any of the above. He took a long swig of his beer, then set it down.

"Don't oversimplify this. It isn't just about sex. I care for Kendra. I always will. More importantly, this is a chance for Kai to finally have his parents living together under one roof. Just like we did."

Vi's expression softened and her shoulders relaxed. "Nate, don't get your hopes up. Kendra's only going to disappoint you again."

Nate cringed at the pity in his twin sister's eyes. "Don't look at me like that, Vi."

"Like what? Like I'm your sister who loves you? It's always been my job to look out for you."

"I don't need you to protect me from Kendra or anyone else, and I certainly don't need your pity. You can pack up all that attitude and take it back with you to wherever you came from." He thrust his thumb over his shoulder and gave her his I-ain't-got-time-for-the-bullshit face.

"First, you know exactly where I came from—Barbados. Second, it was Marcus, Mitchell and Drew's job to protect you from other people. My job is to protect you from yourself. We both know you can be your own worst enemy." She raised an eyebrow and twisted her mouth in a smug smirk when he didn't respond. "Like when you run your big mouth on video at a club in the middle of the night and screw up your contract negotiations."

Nate gritted his teeth. If his own family was going at him this hard, he could only imagine what his first TV appearance—scheduled for later that week—would be like. "It was stupid, shortsighted. I know that, but I can't change what happened. Kendra has a thoughtful strategy laid out, which we're executing now."

"'Executing strategy,' huh?" She used air quotes. "Is that some cute new euphemism for screwing your client?" Vi grabbed a beer out of the freezer.

Nate swiped the beer from Vi's hand before she could open it. "You won't be needing this. You were just about to leave."

"But I smell lasagna, and I'm starving."

"Got it at Maxine's Kitchen." He reached into his wallet and held out a twenty. "Stop and pick yourself up one on the way home. My treat."

"You're kicking me out for her? Really?"

Nate glowered silently, extending the bill.

"I don't need your money." She pointed a finger at him, then sighed, snatching the bill from between his fingers. "But I'll take it anyway. And you should take my unsolicited advice. If you must work with her, keep it professional, before you do something else you'll regret."

Nate grabbed his beer and drained it, hoping his opinionated twin sister wasn't right.

Ms. Thing here doesn't have your back. She never did.

A cavalcade of emotions rolled through her chest as Vi's words replayed in Kendra's head. Anger at Vi's insistence she couldn't be trusted. Gratitude for Nate's staunch defense of her.

Ending up in Nate's bed, in the midst of dealing with the biggest crisis of his career, certainly didn't make her case for being a professional who could be trusted with the fate of his future.

Kendra got up and quickly got dressed. What hurt

the most was Vi's implication that she'd hurt Nate before, and she'd hurt him again.

She couldn't do that to him, and she wouldn't give him false hope.

Once Kendra heard Vi's car leave, she made her way down to the kitchen where Nate was preparing their plates. "Smells delicious."

Nate looked up, disappointed. "I hoped to find you in the same state I left you." He winked, giving her a sly smile.

"I know, but Vi has a point. You're my client, and I don't… I mean… I've never gotten involved with a client before. It's unprofessional and completely unacceptable. I violated our agreement, and I'm sorry. If you want to fire me, I'll understand. Just stick to the plan and execute it. You'll be fine."

Nate waited patiently, his arms folded, until she was finished. "Why would I want to fire you?"

Her heart raced as she forced her eyes to meet his. "Because this can't happen again. That may make things awkward between us, and I don't blame you for not—"

"Look, I'm sorry about Vi busting in here like that. Whether or not we work together…sleep together…it's none of Vi's business or anyone else's."

Kendra ran her fingers through her hair. "You know she's going to tell Marcus and probably your parents. God, your entire family will know by morning."

Nate shrugged. "What difference does that make? Doesn't change how I feel. I'm not sorry about what happened between us. Neither are you." He cupped her cheek.

For a moment, she settled into his palm before logic kicked in.

This is how the whole thing started.

She shook her head and took a step back. "We can't. I'm sorry."

Nate sighed. "Fine, but I'm not firing you. Awkward or not, I expect you to fulfill your end of the contract."

Kendra stood straight and cleared her throat. "Of course."

"And I don't see any reason we can't sit down like two rational adults and have dinner together."

Kendra held her breath, the muscles in her back and shoulders tense. Sitting down to a meal and pretending everything was okay, when what she really wanted was to let Nate take her back to his bed, would be torturous. But he'd gone through all the trouble of making her favorite meal.

"On one condition."

Nate raised a brow as he put salad greens into two bowls. "And that is?"

"We can talk about the campaign, your career, Kai, the weather…anything but us or what happened here tonight. It was a lapse in judgment. I just want to get past it."

Nate shrugged. "Fine."

His tone said anything but *fine*. Still, he'd agreed to her terms.

Kendra released a breath and nodded. They could get through this. Get things back on track. She would deliver the results she promised, then things would go back to the way they were.

She'd be miserable, missing him and regretting the day she walked out of his life.

Chapter 14

Nate straightened his tie and inhaled. They'd be live on the air for his first television appearance since the video went viral in five...four...three...two...one...

He pressed his lips into a smile as he gave his attention to the host of the show. He'd always considered John Chase to be a blowhard who knew incredibly little about the sports he reported on.

Being a guest on the John Chase show wouldn't have been his first choice. But as Kendra pointed out, it was one of the most-watched daytime shows on the major sports network. The ratings were through the roof. Most important, Kendra felt John was fair and that he'd keep his word and not discuss the video.

That remained to be seen. There was something in the guy's eyes that Nate didn't trust.

Then again, when did he trust any reporter?

John welcomed Nate to the panel, then began the discussion. Nate followed the rhythm of the panel's conversation about the stellar numbers the Ontario Badgers wide receiver Dean Carson was putting up in the play-offs after his recovery from an ACL injury nearly a year earlier. The same injury he'd sustained three years ago.

John seemed to sense his hesitance. He asked Nate a pointed question. Within a few minutes, Nate was so engrossed in the conversation, he stopped thinking incessantly about the camera, the millions of viewers in the audience and whether John Chase would ask about the video. Instead, he recounted his own come-back from an ACL tear and praised Dean Carson for his play-off performance.

He settled into easy banter with John and the other two members of the panel—both retired pro football players he admired and respected. Once he relaxed and focused on the topic, his eight minutes on the segment went by quickly.

John wrapped up the discussion with a promo for next week's show. "Join me next week when we discuss the impact of the social media age on pro athletes. Something my man Nate here knows more than a little about. If you've got the time, Nate, I'd love to have you back to get your view on the topic."

Shit.

The son of a bitch offered him an open invitation to talk about his social media disaster in great detail on his very next show.

He opened his mouth to tell John Chase exactly what he thought of his lame move when Kendra caught his eye.

She shook her head almost imperceptibly, then gave him an encouraging smile. He inhaled, then forced a chuckle. "It's a topic I've learned quite a bit about in the past couple of weeks. Unfortunately, my schedule won't permit."

John grinned, tapping the desk. "Fair enough. Just know, you've got an open invitation to come on the show and share more of your analysis of what the Marauders must do to become an elite team in this league." He added, "For the record, I thought everything you said was on the money, and I think it's despicable to secretly film someone and then use the footage to get your fifteen minutes of fame."

John Chase signed off, wishing the audience a good weekend, and then the cameras faded to black.

Nate snatched off the microphone clipped to the lapel of his suit jacket, but before he could stand, Kendra pinned him in place with her gaze. Her eyes pleaded with him to be cool.

He sighed, acknowledging her plea with the slight nod of his head.

"Nate, thanks again for coming on the show." John was standing in front of him, his hand extended. "And thanks for being such a good sport. My viewers would've slaughtered me if I hadn't addressed the issue at all. Tried to do it in a way that would cause minimal discomfort…for both of us."

Nate reluctantly shook the man's hand. "Appreciate that, John. Thank you for having me on the show."

"My pleasure." He turned to talk to one of the other panelists, but then quickly turned back. "By the way, I'm serious about having you back to talk more about what happened that night or your thoughts on the Marauders. Good luck with your contract negotiations."

Maybe John Chase isn't so bad after all.

"Excellent segment." Kendra fell in line beside him as he made his way back to the green room to retrieve his things. "That didn't kill you, now did it?"

It didn't, but he wasn't ready to concede so quickly. "Thought he wasn't supposed to address the video?"

"We agreed he wouldn't make it a topic of discussion in this segment. Clearly, he found a way to skirt the agreement. Thankfully, he did it in a way that was sympathetic and hopefully made viewers sympathize with you, too. Good job on sticking to the script with your response." She followed him into the green room. "And thank you for the way you handled the conversation afterward. John is someone we want as an ally."

"Sure. Anything else?" He lifted his leather satchel onto his shoulder.

She shook her head. "Not until the afternoon taping of that top ten segment for the late-night show. It should be super quick. In and out. Here's the script. It's like three lines." She handed a printed email to him.

Nate reviewed it quickly, then stuffed it in the inside pocket of his suit jacket. "Great. I'll meet you at the studio."

She looked stunned. "Okay, see you then, I guess."

Nate headed out of the studio and into the sunshine on a lovely winter morning in LA.

Nate made his way up the walkway. Jason Hernandez—the Marauders' best tight end and one of his closest friends—was an uncomplicated guy. His place in Cerritos reflected that. The decor was simple and casual, yet attractive. The place was warm and cozy. Someplace you could hang out and drink beer without worrying about staining the furniture or breaking an expensive vase.

Jase had invited Nate over for an early lunch between studio appearances. Before Nate could ring the doorbell, Jase opened the front door, his goofy trademark grin plastered across his face. He was more tanned than usual. "I can't leave you alone for five damn minutes without you stirring up shit."

Nate gave Jase a one-armed hug. "Thought you abandoned me. Tried calling you several times."

"Sorry about that, man." Jase's cheeks and forehead reddened. He retrieved a couple of beers from the fridge. He handed one to Nate. "Went camping and shut off my phone. After that loss, I needed to be alone for a while."

"That place with the luxury tree houses in Oregon?" Nate tilted his head, assessing his friend's quick nod as his gaze raked the floor. There was something Jase wasn't telling him. "Not exactly roughing it."

Jase shrugged. "Wasn't that loss punishment enough?"

"Can't disagree with that." Nate screwed the top off his icy beer. "Still, you and Vi picked a hell of a time to go AWOL."

"Vi's missing?" Jase rearranged the plastic fruit in the bowl on his kitchen counter.

"I wish. After being out of touch for two weeks, she shows up at my place at the worst possible time." Nate took a swig of his beer.

Jase smirked and sipped his beer, too. He sat on a bar stool. "Does that mean what I think it means?"

Nate ran a hand over his head. "Yep."

Jase chuckled, shaking his head. "That twin sister of yours is a little *loca*." They both laughed. "But she loves you and she always has your best interest at heart."

"Maybe she doesn't know what's in my best interest." Nate frowned, returning his beer to the counter. "Maybe she should back off. Let me decide what's best for me."

Jase cocked his head, his dark eyes assessing him. "In the end, it's your choice. You know that. Not like you listen to Vi anyway, unless you agreed with her to begin with."

Nate raised a brow, narrowing his gaze at his friend. "You sound just like her."

Jase cleared his throat and turned to face the bar. He took another sip of his beer. "Maybe that's because it's the truth."

"Hey, if I wanted to hear more of Vi's point of view, I'd be talking to her right now, instead of you." Nate shoved his friend's shoulder.

"So what do you want to hear?" Jase swigged his beer.

Nate shrugged. "Maybe I want you to tell me I'm not *loco* for trying to get back with my ex."

"Hmm…" Jase nodded sagely. "So it was you and Kendra Vi walked in on the other day?"

"How'd you know—"

"I haven't had that many concussions." Jase tapped his right temple twice with two fingers. "Besides, I saw Kendra in the press conference footage. She's handling your PR?"

Nate nodded. "Marcus's idea. I was against it at

first, but it was a good call. Kendra's the right person for the job."

"Speaking of which, how's the apology tour going?"

Nate groaned. "According to Kendra, it's going well. Still, this whole thing has been a shit storm."

"Of your own making." Jase pointed the neck of his beer bottle in Nate's direction. "How many times I gotta tell you, man, you don't have to say everything that pops in your head."

"I don't pull punches. You know that."

"This time, you should have. What were you thinking? Especially in a contract year?"

"I know, I know." Nate stood in front of the window overlooking the pool in the backyard. "I screwed up. Big-time."

"Not the first time. Doubt it'll be the last." A half smirk lit Jase's eyes.

"You're having way too much fun with this." Nate pointed a finger at his friend. "And thanks for the vote of confidence."

Jase chuckled. "You're usually the one riding us out there on the field. Not a chance in hell I'd pass on the opportunity for a little payback."

Nate raised his hands, his palms facing his friend. "Point taken. Now, stop avoiding the question. Am I crazy to want Kendra back?"

"Of course not. She's Kai's mother, and it's obvious you still care for her."

"But…?"

"But, the fact that you care what I think tells me Kendra isn't as sure about this as you are. I'm hoping for the best, but I can't help worrying that you'll be disappointed." Jase shrugged.

Nate surveyed the landscape in the backyard. It was a valid concern. One he shared.

Even if he could get Kendra to give them another try, could he trust that she wouldn't walk away from him again?

He closed his eyes, a shudder moving down his spine.

God, I hope so.

Chapter 15

Kendra paced in the green room of the late-night show. Nate was scheduled for taping in less than half an hour and he wasn't answering her calls.

A wave of sadness rolled over her. The way he'd taken off after the panel this morning…had he gone to see someone else? Was he with her now?

She shook her head to clear it. Who Nate Johnston was with was none of her business, as long as he wasn't doing anything that would further tarnish his brand.

There was a giggle in the hallway, followed by a deep chuckle. Kendra recognized both laughs. The giggle was that of an intern who'd been hovering, hoping to meet Nate. The chuckle indicated she'd finally found him.

Kendra opened the door, and they both looked at her abruptly. "I was beginning to think you'd forgotten how to answer your phone."

There was a gleam in Nate's eye. He smiled and signed the back of the T-shirt the intern was wearing before slipping past Kendra into the green room.

She inhaled, taking a moment to calm herself. "You were supposed to be here half an hour ago."

"You know how traffic is in LA. Besides, I called the studio on my way here. A quick touch-up in the makeup chair and I'm good."

He'd called the studio, rather than calling her? She gritted her teeth, placing a fist on her hip. "And you've been drinking."

He adjusted his tie. "Relax. I had a couple of beers over lunch. Besides, you're my media consultant, not my mother."

Heat crawled up her neck and exploded in her cheeks. She folded her arms and exhaled, straining to keep her voice even. "But it is my job to dig you out of the PR hole you created for yourself and to make sure you don't dig it any deeper."

Nate narrowed his gaze at her. "Your concern is noted, but everything is fine. So just take a deep breath. Your dog and pony show will go on as scheduled."

Despite her blood boiling, she didn't acknowledge the dig.

Nate was trying to get a rise out of her. He was obviously hurt and angry about her decision to pull away.

Kendra silently counted to ten, her fists clenched. She bit back the angry words she wanted to say, her tone neutral. "Our plane leaves in a few hours. I thought maybe we could grab a bite while I catch you up on the appearances scheduled for the next few weeks."

"Actually, I may have other plans after the show." His gaze held hers.

"Oh, well, maybe on the plane—"

"I was hoping to catch a few winks on the plane. It's been an exhausting few days." He folded his arms tightly against his broad chest. His head tilted as he assessed her. Nate was being a world-class ass, but there was something in his warm brown eyes that still melted her heart. Made her want to kiss him.

"Kara will email the updated itinerary to you along with my notes."

"Great." Nate shifted his gaze toward the door. A wide smile spread across his face when the intern peeked her head in to let them know that makeup was ready for him. He indicated he'd be there shortly, then turned back to Kendra. "Anything else?"

She shook her head, overwhelmed with a growing sense of envy. Wishing he'd look at her the way he looked at that intern just now. Her stomach dropped to her knees. "Have a good show."

Something in his demeanor softened. He headed across the room, turning back to look at her over his shoulder. Sadness lurked behind his dark eyes as he opened his mouth to speak, but then he turned and left instead.

Kendra fought back the tears that prickled her eyes, her heart thumping against her chest.

Nate closed the green room door behind him and exhaled.

What an ass.

He'd only meant to be distant. Maybe make her jealous by appearing to eat up the attention of the far-too-young-and-shallow intern. Instead he'd come off as bitter and angry, and he'd been a total jerk.

She maintained her cool, and he was left feeling worse than ever. That's what he deserved for playing childish games.

He wanted to be with her and Kai. Couldn't she see that he was sincere?

Nate tried to shake off the melancholy that settled over him when he saw the pain in Kendra's eyes, despite her forced smile.

He forced a smile of his own as he made his way through a quick turn in the makeup chair, then a brief meeting with the producer and the host of the show.

He fought his way through filming, sporting the broadest smile he could muster. It took a few takes, but finally everyone was satisfied with his performance and he was on his way back to the green room.

"How'd it go?" Kendra greeted him warmly, as if he hadn't been a complete jerk less than an hour ago.

"Pretty well." He grabbed a bottle of water off the table and opened it, ignoring the urge to apologize and admit that he had no interest at all in the intern. "Should get a laugh."

"Great." Her smile rose no higher than the edges of her mouth. Not even close to her genuine smile. The one that rounded the apples of her cheeks, lit her brown eyes and went straight to his heart. "Guess I'll grab a bite, then meet you on the plane."

"Wait, Kendra, I was thinking about your suggestion that we get something to eat and go over things…"

"Yeah?"

"How about we grab dinner, but leave the shop talk at the door. I think we both deserve a break from it, don't you?"

One side of her mouth curved, her eyes dancing. "Are you asking me out to dinner, Nate Johnston?"

"Yeah, I guess I am."

A genuine smile lit her face. "Thought you'd never ask."

"That was incredible." Kendra finished the last bites of her London broil and creamed spinach and then put her fork down.

Nate, who had already finished his culotte steak and lobster tail, leaned back against the booth and grinned. "Told you you'd love this place."

"I had my doubts." The iconic Koreatown steak house looked like a throwback to the 1950s. Dark wood paneling on the walls; comfy, lived-in red leather booths; and crisp white tablecloths lent to the feeling of being transported to the set of an old Rat Pack movie. "But you were right. Thank you for dinner."

"Hate to rush you away after such an amazing meal." Nate stuffed some bills inside the vinyl guest check holder and thanked their server. He helped Kendra into her coat. "But we've got a plane waiting for us."

"No, it's fine." Kendra smiled. "But this was really nice. Much better than the sandwich I had at the commissary."

"About that…" Nate extended his elbow and Kendra slipped her arm through his. "I was a jerk earlier. It won't happen again."

"It's forgotten." She gave him a small smile. After they were both settled in the car, she added, "Hope you had a nice lunch date."

"I did." Nate held back a grin. She was fishing for

information about who he'd spent those missing hours with. "Jase Hernandez invited me out to his place for lunch."

"Oh, well, that sounds nice." She sounded relieved. "And on the subject of invitations… I have one for you. Maya and I are taking the kids to the Pleasure Cove roller-skating rink tomorrow."

"Are you kidding me? Is that old place still out on the edge of town?"

"Yeah, and I'm pretty sure there is still gum stuck underneath the benches from when we were kids."

"Don't look at me, it was Q who had the fascination with sticking his gum everywhere," Nate chuckled, referring to his youngest brother, Quincy.

"So?" She looked at him expectantly, her eyes beaming. "What do you say? I know you can't get out there and skate, especially while you're in the middle of contract negotiations, but you can keep me company while I cheer Kai on from the sidelines. That'll give me an excuse to stay off the skates."

"Well, when you put it that way, how can I possibly refuse?" He grinned. "Just tell me the time and I'll meet you there."

"Great. And I know it's my weekend with Kai, but after skating, he can spend the rest of the weekend with you, if you'd like."

"I would, thank you." A sense of warmth and gratitude filled his chest. "He's been dying to show off his new swimming skills."

"Perfect." She opened her portfolio.

"Hey, if you don't have any plans this weekend, you're welcome to stay, too. We could make it kind of a family thing."

"I don't know." Head tilted, she assessed him, then exhaled. "I don't think it's a good idea for me to spend the night, but I wouldn't mind coming over after the skating rink. I'll even cook. After all, I owe you dinner."

"Sounds nice." It wasn't what he'd hoped for, but at least it wasn't a flat refusal. "But I've got one more request."

"Okay." She regarded him warily.

"This temporary moratorium on discussing business…let's maintain it until Monday morning." He turned toward her. "I'd like to relax, enjoy our time with Kai and forget about the rest of the world. Just for the weekend."

"I know this has been a lot to deal with." Her smile radiated warmth and understanding. "So barring any crisis, you've got yourself a deal."

It was a small victory, but one he savored. The first step to winning Kendra back.

Chapter 16

"Look at me, Dad!" Kai called out gleefully, zipping past Nate and Kendra as he circled the roller-skating rink ahead of his Aunt Maya and cousins Sofie and Ella.

"You're doing great, son!" Nate cheered Kai on, wishing he could join him. The smell of rental skates, stale popcorn, burnt hotdogs and frozen pizza made him nostalgic for the old days.

"Watch where you're going, honey!" Kendra called after him, leaning over the carpeted half wall that separated them from the rink.

"Relax, Dray. He'll be fine." Nate massaged the tension in her shoulders. "Remember how much fun we had out there as kids?"

"It was the place to be on Saturday nights. Every teen in town was here. Oh, and remember the all-night skates?"

"We were dead on our feet by the end of the night." Nate grinned.

The DJ played "Bounce, Rock, Skate, Roll" by Vaughan Mason & Crew and they both cheered, dancing with their hands in the air.

"This song is older than we are." Kendra laughed.

"And it's still the reigning champ of roller-skating songs." Maybe he couldn't put on skates and get out on the wooden floor, but he could dance to his heart's content with his feet on solid ground.

"Every time I hear this song, it's like I'm fifteen all over again." She moved her hips and rocked her head.

"You're showing out now, girl. I need to step up my game." He threw in some popping and locking and added a spin for good measure. "Get it, Dray!"

"Oh, it's on." She pursed her lips, going old school.

"You did not just go TLC on me with the Bart Simpson. Okay, I got one for you."

"Old-school running man!" She laughed. "All right now. How about this?"

They challenged each other with every old-school dance move they could remember: the Humpty dance, the Roger Rabbit, the Cabbage Patch.

"Okay, time to bring it home." He launched into the Kid 'n Play and she joined him until the song finally ended and they collapsed on one of the carpeted benches, both laughing.

"That was so much fun." She panted, catching her breath. "But now I need a rubdown, a soft pretzel and a nap, in that order."

"I can help with all three." He wriggled his eyebrows and laughed.

Watching Kendra grind her hips to the music sped

up his pulse far more than the physical exertion had. He surveyed the space. The walls had been repainted in a cobalt blue and new carpeting covered the floor and walls, but the place was essentially the same.

"We had so many great times in this building, but what I remember most is the first time I kissed you right over there." He pointed to a dim corner of the rink. "Remember that?"

"How could I forget my first kiss?" Her gaze was soft as her eyes met his.

Nate smiled and leaned in closer, whispering in her ear. "Hopefully, I'm a much better kisser now than I was back then."

"I don't know, you were a pretty good kisser back then, too." She grinned. "Aside from that incident when you nearly chipped my tooth."

"My bad." He grinned, his gaze on her sensuous lips as he leaned toward her. "Is it too late to ask for a do-over?"

"Hey, Dad, I'm hungry. Can we get pizza?" Kai skated toward them on the carpeted surface.

"Absolutely, champ." Nate did his best not to sound as disappointed as he felt, but Kendra seemed relieved not to have to answer his question.

Kendra exhaled, thankful Kai had interrupted them before she got caught up in the nostalgia of strolling down memory lane with Nate.

It was the first time they'd both let down their guard, been themselves and simply enjoyed each other's company.

She'd missed that. The laughter, the silliness, the fun and the love.

She wanted that again, but it wasn't that simple. His career and her family's past made it complicated. And she wouldn't hurt him again.

Between working together and her promise to allow Nate to be more involved in Kai's life, she'd have to learn to keep it together. Starting now.

Needing to talk to Maya, Kendra stood and turned to head to the other side of the rink, but she crashed into a woman.

"I'm so sorry, I didn't mean to—"

"No worries. It's Kendra, isn't it?"

She took in the tall brunette, whose dark eyes carefully assessed her. Stephanie Weiss, the reporter who orchestrated the video.

What the hell is she doing in Pleasure Cove?

"You know exactly who I am, Stephanie." Kendra folded her arms. "Here to dig under rocks for more dirt?"

"Guess Nate didn't give you the best impression of me." She almost sounded hurt, but her sarcastic expression indicated otherwise. "That's not my intention. I'm only here to get the real story behind Nate's comments that night. Something beyond that canned speech he served up the other day."

"So why approach me?"

"You're his media consultant. Your client wouldn't consider my offer to give him a chance to explain himself, so I thought I'd make my pitch to you. Perhaps you can make him understand why doing so is in his best interest."

"I'm aware of your offer, and I don't believe it is in his best interest. So if you'd excuse me…"

"It was a peace offering." Stephanie's tone grew

sharper. She pressed her lips into a hollow smile. "One I'm extending again to you."

"No, thank you, and I'd appreciate it if you'd stay away from me and my client. Neither of us has anything else to say to you."

"Suit yourself." Stephanie laughed bitterly, then turned to walk away. She paused, then turned back, a devious grin lighting her eyes. "Did Nate tell you he and I dated?"

"Of course." Every muscle in Kendra's body tensed. "I also know how the relationship ended and that it killed your career."

Stephanie's expression grew bitter for a moment, but then she smiled. "I'm sure that's what he told you, but the truth is, we've known each other intimately since his rookie year with the Marauders." She looked beyond Kendra, to where Nate stood, holding a tray of food. Kai stood beside him. "But I'm sure you've told her all about that. Right, Nate?"

"Stephanie, what the—" Nate started, then looked down at Kai watching him with wide eyes. He cleared his throat, seething. "I told you to stay away from me. I didn't think I needed to tell you that includes my family. Do I need to take legal action for you to get the point?"

A grin spread across the woman's face, her gaze shifting from Nate to Kendra. "Sounds like a man with something to hide."

Kendra's blood grew cold. Her fists clenched and her nails dug painfully into her palms as Stephanie flipped her dark brown extensions over her shoulder and sashayed away in red-bottomed heels.

"Who was that lady, Mommy?" Kai asked, clench-
ing his huge plastic cup of frozen lemonade.

"No one you need to worry about, little man," Nate
said quickly. "Mommy and I need to talk, so let's get
you set up at the table with Auntie Maya and the girls.
Mommy and I will be over when we're done."

Nate escorted Kai to where Maya sat, looking worried. She'd obviously witnessed the exchange between
them and Stephanie Weiss.

He quickly returned to her side. "Babe, I'm sorry
about that. You shouldn't have to deal with her."

"Don't call me *babe*." Kendra's hands shook and
her pulse raced.

Nate frowned. "You don't actually believe that bull,
do you?"

Kendra met his gaze, but didn't respond.

"She's a notorious liar. You said so yourself."

"I never said she was a liar." Kendra spoke slowly,
her voice soft. "I said she was untrustworthy. She'll
use any means necessary to find out the darkest, ug-
liest truths about people. Anything that will advance
her career, no matter how devastating it is to the person. Like what she reported about your friend. It wasn't
untrue, it was just something private that he preferred
the rest of the world not know."

"It's more than that. If a story isn't salacious enough,
she'll put a spin on it, like she's doing right now."

"So there is some truth to what she's saying about
you and her during your rookie year."

She shouldn't care. They weren't together anymore.
So why did it feel like her heart was about to explode?

"Why don't you just go ahead and ask me what

you really want to know?" Nate narrowed his gaze, his voice tight.

"Because I might not like the answer, that's why." Kendra's voice faltered. She exhaled. "Besides, I can't afford the distraction from the question I *need* to have answered."

"Which is?" Nate's incredulous expression indicated that he couldn't believe there was anything more pressing than the issue at hand.

"What the hell is she doing here?"

Nate sighed, realization in his eyes. He knew enough of Stephanie Weiss to recognize that she hadn't come all this way without something sinister in mind.

"What do you think she's planning?"

"I don't know." Kendra shrugged. "But that's where our focus must lie. Not on what happened between you two eight years ago."

"I thought you said you needed to know everything, so we don't get blindsided?" He shoved his hands in his pockets.

"So you didn't tell me the whole truth about you two?" Her mouth felt dry and tears pricked her eyes.

Nate exhaled and sat on a bench, pulling her down beside him. He turned his body to face her, his eyes barely meeting hers.

"Midway through that first season, I'd become this breakout star. Stephanie interviewed me for her sports magazine over dinner. We had a few drinks. I walked her back to her hotel and…she kissed me."

Kendra screwed her eyes shut against the pain in her chest. She blinked back tears. "So did you—"

"Nothing happened, I swear." He held his hands up, his palms facing her. "I told her I don't get down like that. That I was with someone I loved and was going to marry."

"Then why didn't you tell me?"

"I was ashamed of myself for letting it happen."

"You know about my dad, about what he did to our family." She pointed a finger at him.

"*That's* why I was so afraid to tell you the truth." A vein was visible in his temple as he lowered his gaze. "With your history with your father, I was afraid you'd never trust me again. I wasn't willing to take that chance."

"Guess my concerns about what happens out there on the road aren't so unfounded after all." Kendra stood, angrily wiping away the wetness at the corners of her eyes. "Don't worry, this won't change anything between us. I'm still your media consultant, and I will honor my promise to let you spend more time with Kai, because it's the right thing to do. But I don't think it's a good idea for me to come over after all."

"Kendra, please." He grabbed her hand, but she snatched it from his grip. "It was a mistake, and I know I should've told you, but *nothing* happened. I swear to you. You have to believe me."

"No, I don't. My job is to make everyone else believe you." She bit her lower lip and willed her limbs to stop trembling. "Excuse me, but suddenly, I'm not feeling very well." Kendra grabbed her things and made her way to her car.

She'd been right. Like her father, Nate Johnston couldn't be trusted.

Chapter 17

Nate checked his watch again. The last few days had been stressful. His relationship with Kendra was strained and formal, and Vi was still angry with him, so talking to her wasn't an option.

He felt badly for keeping the truth from Kendra. Maybe he hadn't slept with Stephanie that night, or done anything to overtly encourage the kiss, but he'd lapped up the adoration she'd been pouring on all night. And he hadn't discouraged her flirting. Worst of all, he'd kept it from Kendra.

Nate had convinced himself that not telling Kendra was in *her* best interest. The truth was he should've handled the situation differently. Most important, he couldn't bear for her to look at him and judge him as being no better than her father. By hiding it from her, he'd proven just that.

"Sorry to keep you waiting." Bud Flynn placed a firm hand on his shoulder as he took his seat at the table. The older man adjusted his large glasses and smiled through a sigh. "So, how've you been, son?"

"Well, thanks." Nate would've found it demeaning had anyone else referred to him that way. But Bud Flynn had been as good to him as his own father. He'd given him a shot in the league when no one else would. He mentored him through injuries, slumps and tough times—like his breakup with Kendra. "Look, Bud, I want to begin by saying again how sorry I am about this entire mess. I never intended any of this."

"Yet here we are, dealing with it just the same." Once a staple on the sidelines during games and practice, Bud hadn't been as active with the team as he once had due to health issues. It was the first time Nate had ever looked at the old man and seen his eighty-plus years in his blue eyes and bearing down on his shoulders. "You've always been straightforward and outspoken, and I appreciate that. Reminds me a lot of myself."

"Thank you, sir." Nate squirmed in his seat, the shadow of the other shoe Bud was about to lower loomed over him.

"However, there comes a time when you have to learn to control those impulses. Know when to be open and when to season your words up a bit."

"I just got so caught up in my anger with the guys, with myself. It was a mistake to talk about it outside our walls. I'm clear on that now."

A server came, left glasses of water and then took their orders before taking off again.

"It's good you understand that." Bud took a sip from

his water glass. "However, I'm gonna need you to apply that behind closed doors, too."

"Sir?"

"When I was a boy, we didn't have much. My mother made do with what we had. She often bought liver because she could get it cheap and it's good for you. A super food. But if you don't prepare it just right, it's one of the most god-awful things you'll ever eat."

"Okay." Nate assessed the old man, wondering if he was beginning to lose it.

Bud leaned forward, his elbows on the table. "Consider your words the same way, son. What you're saying is a hard truth your coaches and teammates need to hear. But if you don't season those words up just right and make them palatable, they won't do anybody a bit of good. They'll block out every word and use your poor delivery as reason to discount your advice. They'll be so focused on how you told them that they won't pay attention to the wisdom you're offering."

"Point taken." Nate nodded, tapping his thumb on the table. "Kendra told me pretty much the same thing."

Bud smiled. "Caught a glimpse of her at the press conference. She was good for you. Glad to see you two have worked things out, for your sakes and the sake of your son."

Nate lowered his gaze and drew circles in the condensation of his glass. "I've hired her as my media consultant. As for our personal relationship...we're still working on that. She's a little gun-shy."

"Why?" The old man shoved his glasses up the bridge of his crooked nose.

Nate sighed. "She believes every man out there will

disappoint her like her father did. He left them when Kendra was a baby."

"Does she have a good relationship with her father now?"

"She can barely tolerate being in the same room with him."

"Then start there," Bud said matter-of-factly, then thanked the server for the whiskey smash she handed him.

"What do you mean?" Nate took a sip of his imported beer.

"Help her repair her relationship with her father. Seems like that's the only way she'll let go of that fear and anger and move forward."

He'd met Curtis Williams—Kendra's father—once or twice while they were growing up. It was apparent neither of them liked the other. Nate resented Mr. Williams for abandoning Kendra, Dash and Ms. Anna. Mr. Williams clearly didn't trust his daughter's male best friend. He hadn't seen or talked to the man in years. "Thanks, Bud. I'll consider it."

"Good. Now, there's something else I need you to consider, so take a deep breath. Really think about this request before you reject it out of hand."

Nate's spine stiffened. "I get the feeling I should have ordered something a little stronger." He hailed the server and asked her to bring him a Cuba libre, then turned back to his mentor. "Let's hear it."

Bud twisted his mouth, spreading his hands on the table in front of Nate. "We need to think of the future of the team here. You're a critical piece of the team right now, as you have been for the past eight years. But we both know you're nearing the end of the ride."

Nate sighed. Bud's words—though true—were like a punch to his gut. They were already looking past him. On to the next big thing. "Does that mean there's no longer a place for me on the Marauders roster?"

Bud waved his hand. "Of course there is. In fact, I want you to take on an even bigger role in the years ahead. We need your skill and talent on the field. However, it's even more important that you help us begin shaping the next generation of wide receivers. Build a team that can win now and into the future."

Nate clenched his jaw, then took a few gulps of his beer. Bud's hands were wrinkled and covered with age spots, yet Nate felt like the relic. "So, I assume you plan to draft a star wide receiver."

"I do." Bud's tone was unwavering and unapologetic. "Doesn't mean I don't respect your talent and understand what a critical role you play on our team. It means I have great reverence for your smarts and ability. So much so, I want to ensure that our future generation of wide receivers has been mentored by the greatest wide receiver we've ever had."

Nate finished his beer and handed his glass off to the server when she set his Cuba libre on the table. He took a gulp of it, letting the chilled cola, dark rum and lime juice slide down his throat. He closed his eyes for a moment, wishing he were on the sandy beach where he first discovered this drink, rather than sitting across from the team's owner essentially telling him he was washed up and more valuable as a mentor than as a player.

"Well?" Bud took a sip of his whiskey smash.

Nate shrugged. "Don't have much of a choice, do I?"

Bud's voice was somber, fraught with disappointment. "We always have choices, son. I just hope you'll take some time and think about my offer and make the best decision. One beneficial to you and the team."

Nate nodded, meeting the old man's gaze. "I'll give your request serious consideration. I promise. I'd like to talk your proposal over with my team first before I commit."

"Of course." Bud nodded, steepling his fingers. "There is one other matter we need to discuss."

Nate's stomach roiled. He gripped his glass. "Okay."

"I need your assurance that you've learned from this experience. That we won't find ourselves in the same position six months down the road. Because if we do, I need you to understand that this conversation will go very differently." Bud raised one of his furry eyebrows, punctuated by unruly gray hairs that pointed in opposite directions.

Nate nodded. "I have, sir. I can assure you it won't happen again."

"Good." A warm smile spread across Bud's face. He looked around. "Now, where is that prime rib? I'm starving."

Nate chuckled, his head swirling. As shaken as he'd been by Bud's proposal about his changing role on the team, his thoughts kept returning to Kendra.

Suddenly, Bud's suggestion didn't seem so bad. Kendra would be angry if he interfered in her relationship with her father, but if Bud was right, it would be worth enduring her temporary ire.

After dinner with Bud, Nate drove back to his place in Memphis. Then he booked a flight to Jacksonville, Florida.

Chapter 18

Kendra sat on the set of another midday sports show as Nate took part in a discussion panel. This time they were in Atlanta.

It was down to two teams that would play for the championship. The absence of football action didn't stem the tide of talking heads analyzing every facet of each remaining team and predicting how the contest would end.

Nate was a natural—funny and charming. His words insightful and his opinions thought-provoking. Initially, he'd been against doing the sports shows. Now he was in his element, loving every minute.

His smile was broad and genuine and his deep chuckle was contagious. Not to mention, the man was finer than he'd ever been.

Kendra massaged the knot in her shoulder and breathed through the heat building in her chest.

It was no use.

Flames marched down her spine, fanning the heat at her core as she tried to clear the memories of the night they'd spent in his bed.

You're the one who rejected him. Twice.

Her anger and distrust aside, she still loved and wanted Nate. But how could she trust him again? And what about her career? He hadn't been supportive of it then, why would things be any different now?

Nate made a funny observation that had the entire panel in stitches.

Kendra smiled. She'd missed hearing his genuine laugh. He'd spent the previous few days in Memphis while she'd been back in Pleasure Cove. They met in New York, where he did a few shows before they'd flown to Atlanta for this one. After another appearance scheduled later in the day, they'd head back to Pleasure Cove.

"How'd I do?" Nate approached her, a sheepish smile turning up the corners of his mouth.

Her eyes traveled the length of his body, draped in an expensive blue suit that enhanced his athletic build. She lifted her gaze to meet his. "You're a natural. You'll have a long career ahead of you as a sports analyst, if that's what you want."

"Think so?" He relieved her of her leather briefcase and lifted it onto his shoulder as they headed toward the door.

"Absolutely. The producers loved you. They asked if you'd like to come back and do a few shows during the off-season."

Nate nodded thoughtfully. "That's great, but let's

hope all of this will pay off at the negotiations table. Marcus is meeting with the team later today."

"If they had no intention of paying you, Bud wouldn't have asked you to mentor James Eastland."

"I guess." Nate's shoulders tensed. He was obviously still unhappy about being asked to mentor a younger player. A sure sign his days with the team were numbered. "How much time until the next show?"

"A few hours. Plenty of time for you to grab a bite or go back to the hotel and get a little rest. I can meet you at the next studio, if you'd like."

"No." He lightly gripped her arm. "Let me take you to lunch, if you don't have any plans."

Kendra's heart beat faster. Her mouth felt dry as she stared into his warm eyes. "Why? Did you want to go over the appearances scheduled for next week?"

"No, we need to talk about us. I'm sorry for my bad judgment then and for not telling you when it happened."

She pulled away. "Nate—"

"I know you'd rather not talk about this." He countered her objection before she could make it. "But that's always been our problem. We've avoided the tough conversations. Maybe that's because we got together so young. Maybe we weren't mature enough to deal with all of this then. But we need to talk about it now."

Nate cupped her face in his strong hand, lifting Kendra's chin so her eyes met his.

Kendra backed up until she was pressed against the wall. Her heart beat so quickly she was sure he could hear it. She stared at him, unable to speak. Her chest was heavy with all the things she wanted to say;

her head spun, reminding her of all the reasons she shouldn't say them.

He captured her mouth in a kiss. Slow and sweet. Filled with warmth, affection and desire. Her hands slipped beneath his jacket, pressing into his back. Her body softened against his.

She was kissing Nate Johnston in a secluded hallway at a major sports network. She'd lost her mind. Yet she had no desire to stop him. Nor would she pretend that she didn't want more.

Kendra pulled away. She bit her lower lip as their eyes met. There was so much they needed to say, but she didn't want to talk. "I know exactly what I'd like for lunch."

A slow smile spread across his face as he traced her collarbone. "What?"

"You." Kendra's heart raced, hardly able to believe what she'd said.

From the widening of Nate's eyes, he could hardly believe it, either. Nate nodded his head toward the door. His voice was a hoarse whisper. "Let's get out of here. Now."

They took the waiting car service back to their hotel, Nate gripping her hand for the short ride.

A quiet, nervous energy buzzed between them as they rode in silence in the back of the black SUV.

Kendra wasn't prepared to think about where they stood or Stephanie's accusation. She simply wanted the comfort and solace she'd only ever felt when she was in Nate's arms.

Nate had planned to apologize to Kendra again and outline all the reasons they belonged together over lunch. But he'd kissed her and then Kendra proposed the very thing he wanted so desperately: to spend the next few hours making love to her.

The temptation too great, he couldn't say no.

When they arrived at the hotel, Nate escorted Kendra to his suite, nearly holding his breath, afraid she'd reconsider.

Once inside, he kissed her. Gripped those heart-stopping curves, hauling them against the hard planes of his body.

Nate sizzled with heat everywhere his skin met Kendra's. He yanked her blouse from the waistband of her skirt, desperate to touch her heated flesh. His hands glided down her back, over the firm curve of her soft behind. He hiked the tight navy skirt as high as he could, giving him better access to the soft, smooth flesh at the back of her thighs. He squeezed one leg, lifting it higher.

"God, I want you." He barely managed to get the words out as he planted kisses down her throat. "I haven't stopped thinking of you since you left my bed."

Nate's long fingers glided over the damp satin material shielding her sex. His need for her spiraled with each sensual murmur escaping her throat. He swallowed her soft moans as she arched her back and tugged his shirt from his pants.

His gaze locked with hers as his chest reverberated from his erratic heartbeat. His breathing ragged, a rush of emotions flooded over him.

Love, admiration and raw desire inflamed by the abject need he saw in her eyes.

Beads of sweat trickled down Nate's back as he stripped Kendra of her suit jacket, letting it fall to the floor. He trailed kisses down her neck, along her collarbones and across her shoulders. Nate inhaled her jasmine and gardenia scent. It was an expensive perfume he'd splurged on before he'd signed his first contract. She'd made it her signature scent. Still wore it after all these years.

Would she still be wearing such a personal gift if she didn't still love him the way he loved her?

Nate dug his fingers into her soft ebony curls and sucked her lower lip between his before exploring her warm mouth—sweet and minty—with his eager tongue. Heat and electricity flowed through his spine, into his fingertips and toes.

No one had ever come close to making him feel the way he did when he was with her. Like he could conquer the world, if only she were by his side.

No one ever would.

Kendra was enticing, but her real beauty lay in the depths beneath her surface. Confident in her abilities, she could go toe-to-toe with anyone. She could be gentle and kind or determined and fierce. And the woman just got sexier with each passing year.

He wanted her body. Admired her mind. Most important, he needed her and Kai in his life.

He loved her. Wanted her so much that the thought of losing her again made his chest ache.

What if he confessed everything in his heart and still she rejected him?

Sweat formed over his brow. His heart, pounding in his chest, was too raw to handle another rejection. His ego couldn't sustain another blow like that.

Kendra seemed to notice his distraction. She stepped just beyond his reach and kicked off her heels. Unfastening the button at her waist, she made a show of slowly tugging down the zipper of her skirt. She kicked aside the material pooled around her ankles.

Standing there in a blue camisole and a silky pair of panties that provided limited coverage for her firm, round bottom, she was breathtaking.

Nate pushed aside the dark thoughts that tormented him and focused on the moment. A moment he'd fantasized about since he'd last had Kendra in his bed. He licked his lips. His pulse raced as Kendra stripped off the camisole.

He reached for his tie, but she tugged him closer by the narrow strip of fabric, loosened it and slid it from his neck. Kendra slipped his jacket from his shoulders, then painstakingly unbuttoned each button of his dress shirt, relieving him of it and the undershirt he wore beneath it.

The corner of her mouth curled in a sexy smirk that hit him below the belt, tightening his length. He restrained the desire to rip off what little remained of her clothing and take her hard and deep. To remind her how perfectly their bodies fit together, and how good he could make her feel.

She'd taken control, and he'd gladly let her have it…for now.

Kendra pressed her warm mouth to his bare chest, laying gentle kisses on his heated flesh. He inhaled at the sensation of her cool tongue grazing his nipple, then swirling around it. She slid her hands down his back and gripped his ass.

He groaned at the glorious sensation of his taut rod pressed between them. She unbuckled his belt, then unzipped his pants.

Kendra tugged her lower lip between her teeth as she scanned the ridge beneath his underwear. She slipped her hand underneath the waistband and curled her warm fingers around his shaft. Pumping it, she elicited involuntary groans of pleasure. Her gaze locked with his as she worked him with her hand until he could barely remember his own damn name.

Conversation was out of the question.

The muscles of his legs and back tensed, pressure building as she brought him closer to release. Nate gently gripped her throat, pressing his open mouth to hers in an effort to wrest back control and slow his ascent to climax.

Kendra released her grip on his painfully hard shaft. Digging her fingers into his back, she sighed softly. Her hands trailed down his back as she gave in to his fervent kisses. Impatient, she shoved his pants and underwear down his hips, freeing his rigid length.

So much for a slow seduction.

He'd planned to take his time. Convey his deepest feelings through each kiss and touch as he made love to her.

His plan dissolved in the rush of adrenaline in his veins.

She'd brought him so close to the edge. He ached for the intense relief he could only find being buried inside her slick walls, his name on her lips.

Nate fumbled to retrieve a condom from his wallet before clumsily shedding his pants and briefs and kicking off his shoes. He sheathed himself, then stripped Kendra of the bra and panties that were the last barrier to the uninhibited glory of her captivating curves.

He lifted her, his arms bracing her legs and her

back pressed against the wall as he drove deep inside her wet heat.

Nate's gaze met hers as he lifted her slowly, then eased her back down until he was fully seated inside her, creating a rhythm. The exquisite sensation was intensified by the call-and-response of Kendra's hushed moans and his soft curses as they accelerated toward bliss.

Her arms around his neck, Kendra pulled his mouth to hers in frantic, hungry kisses that catapulted his spiral out of control.

Muscles tense, he strained with the effort of maintaining his focus as he lifted her higher, then plunged deeper. His movements swifter, more powerful. The sound of her naked skin slapping against his filled the space.

Kendra tensed, her nails scraping his back as she called out his name. Her slick walls spasmed, milking his throbbing flesh as he soared to his own release.

Their hearts still racing, he pressed his damp forehead to hers and held her as they caught their breath.

"That was incredible." He kissed her, then reluctantly released her to the floor, his breathing still ragged. "Can I get you anything?"

She pressed a kiss to his chest. "More of you."

"Can a brother have a sec to recharge?"

Her mouth twisted in a sensuous smirk that tested his will. "Fine, but we're leaving in time for your next show…round two or not."

"Yes, ma'am." He winked, swatting her bottom playfully before heading to the bathroom.

When he returned, Kendra was seated on the bed, the sheet strategically positioned across her body. One foot dangled off the edge of the bed; the other was folded beneath her.

Hair tousled, her cheeks and chest flushed, she was a vision of loveliness. One he wanted in his bed every night, not just in his dreams.

"You're beautiful, you know that?"

She smiled sheepishly, straightening the leg beneath her. "You're pretty handsome yourself."

Nate pulled Kendra to the edge of the bed and knelt between her knees. He trailed a finger down her chest. "You're an amazing woman, Kendra. I'm lucky to have you in my corner."

"And I'm proud of you, Nate. Of the man you've become."

Her sincere expression filled him with warmth. It meant more to him than she could possibly know.

He kissed her. Made love to her. Allowed himself to imagine the joy of never having to let her go again.

Kendra's body hummed with energy and her cheeks were filled with heat. The friction of her taut nipples grazing the fabric of her clothing made it difficult to concentrate.

She fanned herself with a brochure, hoping the producers didn't shush her for making too much noise on the set.

Could everyone else see the glow she felt after leaving Nate's bed less than two hours ago?

Kendra surveyed the crew on the set of the sports talk show. Preoccupied with running the program, they paid her little attention.

Kendra squirmed in the director's-style chair, crossing her legs tightly. Her foot bounced involuntarily.

When she looked up, Nate caught her eye. A mischievous grin animated his handsome face before he returned his attention to the panel's discussion about whether the all-star game should be played before or after the championship game.

Desperate for a distraction, Kendra looked down at her phone. The ringer and alarms had to be silenced when they were on set. She'd missed several calls. She scanned them. It was her sister.

A chill ran down her spine and her fingers suddenly felt cold. Maya wasn't a serial caller. She left a message and waited for her to call back, especially when she knew they'd be on set.

At the next commercial break, Kendra left the set to call her sister.

Maya answered right away. "Kendra, I'm sorry to call you like this. Everything will be fine, but there's been an accident."

She held her breath. "Who?"

"It's Kai, sweetie. He fractured his left arm."

A fleeting sensation of intense pain ran up Kendra's left arm. She could only imagine how Kai must feel. "How did this happen?"

"Liam took the kids to the playground." Maya said after a brief pause. "Kai jumped off the jungle gym. We're so sorry this happened. Liam insists on paying for the surgery."

"Surgery?" Kendra kneaded the back of her neck. A fresh wave of panic swept over her. "Can't they just put on a cast?"

"He fractured the bone between his elbow and wrist in two places. They have to put in pins."

The room seemed to tilt, and her knees nearly gave

way. Kendra sank onto the sofa, her hands shaking. "When are they performing the surgery?"

"They want to do it right away. Liam is trying to delay it until you and Nate arrive. I know he's on air right now, but can you get here as soon as possible? I don't know how much longer it's safe to wait."

"We'll be there as soon as we can. Hold them off as long as possible. I need to see him before he goes into surgery." Kendra wiped her cheeks. She hadn't even realized she was crying. "Kiss Kai and tell him Mommy and Daddy love him and we'll be there as soon as we can."

Chapter 19

Kendra rushed off the elevator on the surgical floor with Nate hard on her heels.

"My name is Kendra Williams. I'm looking for my son, Kai Johnston. He's scheduled for surgery on a broken arm."

The woman tilted her head, her dark eyes narrowing. "I remember you. You were in here with him a few months ago. He knocked out his front teeth."

"Yes." Heat filled Kendra's cheeks. There was something accusatory about the woman's tone. "Can you please tell me where my...our son is?"

"Nate Johnston." The nurse's eyes lit up with recognition. "I saw you on the *Donnie Jones Sports Hour* earlier today."

"That's right." Nate's tone was measured. "Could you please just tell us where we can find our son? We're hoping to see him before he goes to surgery."

The woman seemed miffed at Nate's rebuff. She pointed down the hall. "Check in at the next nurses' station. They can help you there."

Before they made it to the nurses' station, Liam approached them. His tall frame seemed shorter and there were deep furrows across his forehead.

"Kendra, I'm so sorry. We tried to hold them off as long as we could, but the surgeon couldn't wait any longer." Liam's British accent was more pronounced, his voice heavy with distress.

Kendra's heart fell. Kai had gone into surgery without her there to assure him everything would be okay. "Thank you for getting him here so quickly, and for doing what you could. We appreciate it."

She turned back to look at Nate, who was scowling at Liam as if he was considering pounding him into the floor.

She placed a gentle hand on Nate's arm, hoping he received her silent plea. "Nate, this is Maya's fiancé, Liam Westbrook. Liam, this is Kai's dad, Nate Johnston."

Nate didn't extend his hand and Liam didn't force the issue. He simply nodded and repeated his apology to Nate.

"Why was he with you?" Nate folded his arms.

"Kendra's mum had a doctor's appointment, Maya had a big meeting at work today and our nanny has come down with a bug of some sort. I took the day off to care for the children. We went to see an animated film, then they wanted to stop at the playground before we returned to our flat."

Nate grunted. "And exactly how did this happen?"

"Kai climbed atop the climbing frame while the

girls played on the slide. Ella came down the slide too fast and hit the ground. I was tending to her when Kai called out to me, 'Uncle Liam, look what I can do.' He was airborne before I could tell him not to jump. I only turned my head for a minute. It happened so fast. I've gone over it in my head again and again, wondering what I could have done differently."

"Don't." Kendra squeezed Liam's arm. "Boys do crazy things. We ended up here just a few months ago when he fell down the stairs at my mom's house. These things happen."

Liam didn't look convinced.

"And you won't believe the crazy things this one and his brothers did when we were kids." Kendra jerked a thumb over her shoulder in Nate's direction, hoping to loosen up his sour face and genie stance. "He's got quite a collection of scars and broken bones to prove it."

Liam hugged Kendra and sighed. "I still feel absolutely dreadful about it, but I appreciate your kindness. Please, allow me to take care of the medical bills. Kai was in my care at the time—I should be the one to handle it."

"We can take care of our own kid." Nate's words had a sharp edge. "So thanks, but no thanks. We're good."

"Of course." Liam nodded solemnly. "Didn't mean to cause any offense."

"You didn't." Kendra narrowed her gaze at Nate before turning back to Liam and forcing a smile. "We appreciate the offer. Now, can you tell us what the doctor said?"

Kendra slipped her arm through Nate's. He softened his stance, allowing his hand to fall to his side as Liam explained that Kai had Monteggia fractures of the left radius and ulna. Pins would be inserted to hold the bones in place. However, the growth plates weren't affected and he should recover fully after wearing a cast for several weeks.

Nate seemed to breathe easier. He threaded his fingers through hers, and the rapid beat of her heart slowed. She nodded as Nate asked questions, glad to let him handle it.

Once Liam briefed them, he led them to the small private waiting room where their families were gathered.

"You're a great uncle, Liam," Kendra reassured him. "Thank you again for taking care of our son. It could've happened with any of us."

Kendra didn't miss Nate's subtle sneer when she referred to Liam as Kai's uncle.

"Liam, would you tell everyone we'll be there in just a minute? Nate and I need to ask the nurse a question."

Nate raised an eyebrow and frowned. He clearly suspected why she wanted to talk to him.

Nate trudged through the open waiting area and dropped into one of the chairs. He dragged a hand down his face. "What did I do now?"

Kendra stood in front of him with an expression that scolded him like a child. She folded her arms, bringing attention to her chest. He dropped his gaze. Right now he needed to stay focused on their son, not reminisce about what they'd done earlier in the day.

"Why are you being such an ass? Liam loves Kai. He'd do anything for him."

"I don't need him to do anything for my son. Maybe

he's a big shot in merry old England—" Nate feigned a terrible British accent "—but I don't need his charity."

"He didn't mean anything by it. He feels guilty. He only wants to help. That doesn't make him a bad guy."

"It makes him a condescending one."

"If you knew anything about Liam, you'd know he's not like that at all."

"Well, I don't, and I don't appreciate him acting like I can't take care of my own kid. No one asked for his help."

"He's Kai's uncle and your son adores him."

Hearing how much his son adored some other man felt like a punch square in the jaw. He pressed a stream of air through his nose and shook his head. "Maybe if I got to spend as much time with my own kid as he apparently does, Kai would feel that way about me instead of that guy."

Kendra's eyes widened for a moment, then her expression softened, her eyes filled with what he was sure was pity. She released an audible breath, then sat beside him.

She placed a warm hand over his. "I know it's hard not seeing Kai as often as you'd like, but he loves you, Nate. You'll always be his hero."

Nate grunted, his gaze still on the gray hospital floor tiles. "You don't see the glow in his eyes when he talks about Liam the Great."

Kendra shook her head and laughed. "You're being funny, but the truth *is* Liam is pretty great. He's great for my sister. Great for the town of Pleasure Cove. And he's great with the kids—our son included. We should be thankful Kai has a big family of people who love him."

Nate gritted his teeth. The muscles in his jaw tensed. "Shacking up with your sister doesn't make him family."

Lips pursed, Kendra narrowed her gaze. "So you're going to go all 1950s on me? Fine. They're engaged, so he will be soon. But in my book, he couldn't be a better uncle, even if he were blood."

"From what I hear, he hasn't always been so good to his blood brother, either." He huffed, hating that he'd revealed his hand.

Now she'd know he'd talked to his brother Mitchell, who worked as Liam's next in command at Pleasure Cove Luxury Resort—one of the many resort properties owned by Liam's family.

What he hadn't gleaned from Mitchell—or his brother hadn't been willing to reveal—he'd learned by searching the web. Liam had sustained a feud with his brother Hunter for years over a woman Liam had dated and his brother eventually married.

Kendra stood, glowering down at him, her expression filled with disappointment. "People make mistakes, Nate. Hopefully we learn from them and eventually grow up. You should try it."

Nate caught hold of her hand as she turned to walk away. "I'm not trying to be difficult. It's just hard seeing Kai so excited when he talks about this guy. It feels like Liam is trying to take my place in Kai's life."

Kendra's eyes glistened. She cupped his cheek. Her sweet, familiar scent soothed his anxiety, warming his chest.

"Our son is growing up, Nate. New people will constantly come into his life. No matter how much he admires or cares for them, it doesn't mean he doesn't love us, too." She smiled. "You'll always be his number one. Always."

Nate grasped the hand on his cheek and kissed her palm. He slipped his arms around her waist and pulled her closer, pressing his ear to the thumping of her heartbeat.

"Marcus was right. You've always been able to talk me down off the ledge."

She leaned down and kissed his head. "That's why they pay me the big bucks."

Laughter rumbled in her chest, immediately followed by a sharp intake of air. Nate glanced up at her face. The corners of her eyes were wet with tears. He pulled her onto his lap. "What's wrong, babe?"

She shook her head and wiped her eyes with the back of her hand. "Nothing, because Kai is going to be fine, right?"

"Of course he is." He swiped her wet cheek with his thumb. "He's a Johnston. Takes more than a couple of broken bones to take us out."

She nodded, a nervous laugh bubbling from her pursed lips. "He's a warrior. Like his dad."

"There you are." Liam stood in the doorway, his expression a mixture of guilt and relief. "Kai's out of surgery. Everything went brilliantly. The doctor wants to see you now."

Kendra hugged Nate, thanked Liam and headed off in search of the doctor.

Liam shifted his attention to Nate. He cleared his throat. "Again, I can't tell you how sorry I am."

"I know. And about earlier…" Nate sighed deeply. "I'm sorry. I'm not usually that much of an ass. I was just really worried about our son." He extended his hand and shook Liam's firmly. "Thank you for taking care of Kai today."

If he couldn't always be there for his son, it was good to know someone else who cared about him would.

Chapter 20

Kendra's eyes fluttered open in response to the harsh sunlight filtering through Kai's hospital room window. She repositioned herself in one of the comfy recliners and pulled the plush throw up around her neck.

It wasn't her own bed, but the setup was remarkably comfortable. Despite her insistence that it wasn't necessary, she was glad Liam upgraded Kai's room to a family suite so she and Nate could both spend the night there in comfort.

She looked around. Kai was resting peacefully, unbroken limbs akimbo, in his blue-and-white-patterned hospital gown. She moved beside him and leaned down to kiss his forehead.

The door opened and Nate stepped inside carrying a pastry box and a carafe of coffee. From the delicious scent of both, there was no way either item came from the hospital cafeteria.

"That coffee smells delicious, and are those dough-nuts?"

Nate popped the lid open, revealing her favorite doughnuts in the world. Maple bacon, from Lila's Cafe. They'd met there for coffee a few times during the weeks they'd been working together.

"Thank you." She reached into the box and grabbed one. She took a generous bite of sweet, salty perfec-tion. The doughnut was soft and fresh. It melted in her mouth. An involuntarily murmur conveyed her satis-faction.

Nate's eyes widened in response. He cleared his throat. "Got your favorite coffee, too."

"A mint chocolate mocha from Lila's?"

"You know it."

Kendra stood on her toes and kissed his cheek. Cedar and citrus filled her nostrils as she inhaled his fresh-out-of-the-shower scent.

"Is that a maple bacon doughnut?"

Nate and Kendra both turned toward the small, groggy voice coming from their son, his eyes barely open.

Kendra dropped the remainder of the doughnut back in the box and rushed over to him. "Kai, sweetie, you're awake. Don't you ever scare Mommy like that again."

"Hey, champ." His dad sat on the opposite side of the bed and mussed his son's hair. "Didn't we tell you that time you fell down the steps at Nana's that you can't fly?"

Kai swallowed hard and nodded. "This time I wasn't trying to fly. I just wanted to show Uncle Liam how far I could jump down after I climbed up the moun-tain, just like he did."

"Honey, your uncle is an experienced mountain climber. And he didn't just jump off the mountain. He had special equipment and training." Kendra squeezed Kai's hand, ignoring Nate's frown. "So promise Mommy you won't ever try anything like that again."

"I promise."

"Good." She kissed his forehead. "How do you feel?"

"Tired and thirsty and hungry. Can I have some water and a doughnut?"

"Yes and yes." Nate poured a small glass of water. "You want to sit up, li'l man?"

When Kai nodded, Nate picked up the remote and adjusted the bed.

"Cool. Can I play with it?"

Nate and Kendra laughed.

"It's not a toy, honey. It's the remote to the bed," Kendra explained. "Tell you what, you can have your doughnut, but only after you eat a real breakfast. How about some eggs and bacon?"

Kai agreed reluctantly and she called in his breakfast order while Nate found a children's program for him to watch on television, then showed Kai how to work the remote. When she hung up the telephone, Nate was there, frowning at her.

"You want to tell me again how Kai's accident wasn't Captain Awesome's fault? He was probably bragging about his mountain climbing, BASE jumping adventures. No wonder Kai got the crazy idea to jump off the jungle gym."

"Mommy, Daddy…"

"Just a minute, sweetie," Kendra called over her shoulder, then turned back to Nate. "You're being ridiculous. He's a little boy with a vivid imagination.

Just like you and your brothers were. Stop trying to make this Liam's fault. I thought we'd squashed this yesterday."

"But Mommy…"

"Just a sec, champ," Nate said. He lowered his voice and turned back to her. "All I'm saying is maybe this guy is as great as everyone seems to think he is, but that doesn't mean he knows the first thing about taking care of a kid."

"Who does when they first have children? Liam's never had kids before, but he's really good with them." Kendra pointed a finger at Nate for emphasis. "What happened with him is no different than when he fell at my mom's or yours. Not to mention the time he got that knot on his forehead when he was with you in Memphis."

"You're on TV, Daddy."

"I know, champ. That was from yesterday," Nate said.

"Look, there's Mommy, too."

Nate and Kendra both looked toward the screen. There was a picture of her and Kai at the skating rink, then another of her at the press conference.

"Sweetie, turn up the volume, please." Kendra tried to keep her voice calm, despite the fact that her heart was beating like a jackhammer and her legs suddenly felt like jelly.

The news story raised suspicions about Kai's injuries, painting a picture of her as either an abusive mother or a very neglectful one.

"What the hell…?"

"Don't say bad words, Daddy."

"Sorry." Nate rubbed the back of his neck. "Do me a favor and turn back to the cartoons, okay?"

Kai happily complied.

Nate turned to Kendra. "Don't panic, babe. Everything is going to be fine."

"They're making me look like an unfit mother." She clenched her fists as she paced the floor, tears spilling down her cheeks. "Your ex-girlfriend did this."

She couldn't help her accusatory tone. Kendra knew it wasn't fair. Nate didn't ask for any of this.

"She must've had someone at the skating rink taking photos."

"I knew she had it out for me, but I had no idea she'd stoop low enough to involve you." He gripped her shoulders and held her gaze. "Listen to me, Kendra, I promise I'll do whatever it takes to fix this. Everything is going to be fine. All right?"

He hugged her to his chest. Kendra pressed her face to Nate's sweater and melted into him, hoping she could trust him, and that everything would be okay.

Nate paced the floor of his beach house, clutching his cell phone. He'd promised Kendra he would do whatever it took to make this right, and he meant it. Even if it meant dancing with the devil herself.

He forced out a slow breath, then dialed the phone.

There was a smirk in her voice when Stephanie answered. "I wondered how long it would take for you to reconsider my offer."

Nate clenched his teeth and breathed, saying the vile things he thought of Stephanie Weiss in his head, rather than aloud.

"Look, Stephanie, I'm sorry about how things

worked out between us and about what happened with your career. I discredited your story, not because I wanted to hurt you, but because you put me in a position where I had to protect my friend. But what you're doing in retaliation is ruthless and unethical. The Stephanie Weiss I knew was ambitious, but a generally decent human being. What happened to you?"

"I got blackballed from legitimate sports networks, thanks to you." Her tone was icy. "You made me look like a fool in front of the entire world. Don't like it so much when the shoe is on the other foot, do you?"

"I don't care what you say about me, but bringing my family into it… That's low, even for you." Nate tried to keep his voice level.

She clucked her tongue three times. "Not a smart way to talk to the person whose help I assume you're about to request."

He clenched his fist and willed himself to calm down. "Actually, I'm calling to help you. You want people to view you as a legitimate reporter? Start by reporting honestly. Stop creeping around taking pictures of my kid and his mother. She's a genuinely good person and a hell of a mom. She doesn't deserve this."

"And I did?" Stephanie's voice reached a high pitch. "I was sleeping in your bed three nights a week, but you chose your teammate's reputation over mine. Now I'm supposed to feel bad for some baby mama of yours?"

He cringed at the term *baby mama*. "She's my son's mother, and yes, I expect you to behave as if you have a shred of decency." Nate massaged his temple. "Maybe I'm not entitled to privacy, but my kid and his mom, they are."

"You know how this works. Anyone associated with

a public personality is fair game. Now, are you calling just for old times' sake, or have you reconsidered my offer?"

Nate was silent. Appealing to her sense of decency had been a bust—though he'd put little faith in that possibility. Now he scrolled through his remaining options. Give in to her demands or beat her at her own game.

He chose the latter.

"Actually, I'm calling to make you an offer."

"Oh?"

"Lay off me and my family or I swear to you, one day soon, you'll be lucky to get a job at the daily gazette in Bumfuck Nowhere."

She laughed incredulously. "You of all people, Nate, should know I don't respond well to threats."

"You of all people, Stephanie, should know I'm willing to protect my family by any means necessary."

"Then I guess there's nothing more for us to say." Despite Stephanie's bravado, her voice was tentative. "One day you'll look back and wish you'd taken me up on my offer."

"I won't," he said, "but I assure you that you'll wish you'd taken me up on mine." Nate ended the call, then dialed another number.

"This is Edge. What can I do for you, Nate?" Edgerton Mathis, a private investigator often employed by members of the Marauders, always sounded laid-back, like he was drinking a beer and smoking a blunt.

"Remember that dossier I asked you to put together on that reporter a while back?"

"The one you told me to burn because you were afraid of causing irreparable damage to her career?"

Nate swallowed. "Yeah, that's the one. Any chance you can re-create that?"

"Maybe," Edge said. "This have anything to do with that piece running today, implying your ex is a bad mom?"

Nate didn't acknowledge the question. "How long will it take you to put it together?"

"Two hours."

Nate had always suspected that a guy like Edge held on to files like this. He didn't comment on exactly what he thought of that. "Good. You think it's enough to discredit her?"

Edge chuckled. "What I showed you three years ago? That ain't even the half. Been keeping tabs on this one just for the hell of it. With the way she operates, it was only a matter of time until she ended up on someone's shit list again."

"Good. Same as we agreed on last time?"

"Double the content, double the price."

Nate gritted his teeth. Hell, he'd be willing to pay four times what they'd agreed on previously if it would expose Stephanie for the snake she was and help clear the rumors about Kendra. "Fine. There's a generous bonus in it if you use your pipeline to put this info out to the media, rather than having it come from my camp."

"Done." There was a smile in Edge's gritty voice. "I'll send you a text with my account number in the Caymans. Wire half now, the rest after the news hits the airwaves. Then ding dong, the wicked witch's career is dead."

"I'll wire the money as soon as I get the info."

"One more thing," Edge said. "My gut is telling me

Weiss isn't in this alone. If I tug on that thread, it may unravel something you aren't prepared to deal with."

"What do you mean?"

"The person she's colluding with may be a team-mate." There was the clink of ice in a glass in the background. "Maybe even someone you consider a friend."

"I don't believe it." Nate paced the floor. Could one of his teammates have enough malice toward him to jeopardize his career and his family? "But if it's true…"

"It'll be included in the story."

Nate ended the call with Edge and poured himself a shot of whiskey. When the truth came out about Steph-anie's "reporting" methods, she'd be done. She'd be a pariah with whom no reputable news outlet would want ties.

He hadn't resorted to this option three years ago, because despite what Stephanie had done, he'd once cared for her. He hadn't wanted to destroy her career.

But now she'd left him no choice.

His family meant everything to him. He'd do what-ever it took to protect them. Even if it meant Stepha-nie Weiss and her co-conspirator getting what they deserved.

Chapter 21

"Have you seen the news?" There was a lilt in Kendra's voice that he hadn't heard since the reports questioning her parenting abilities hit the airwaves.

"Been preparing for a trip." Nate threw a couple days' worth of socks and underwear in his luggage. "Why, what's up?"

"Stephanie is all over the news. It looks like the Marauders' personnel manager, Lee Davis, conspired with her to compromise your image, so the team wouldn't offer you a new contract."

"Marcus mentioned it," he said nonchalantly. "He suspects that's the reason the Marauders were so quick to offer me such a generous final contract."

"She's been tapping people's phone lines and using a bunch of shady tactics. Plus, it looks like she's been known to falsify sources. It's been going on for years."

"Hmm…" He put the phone on speaker and tossed it on the bed while he rummaged through his nightstand for a few pictures of Kai and Kendra he kept there. "Guess we won't have to worry about her anymore."

Kendra was silent for a moment. "Nate, you didn't have anything to do with this, did you?"

He scratched the back of his neck. "You really want to know?"

"Did you do anything illegal or unethical to make this happen?"

"I did not." He couldn't vouch for Edge, but that was the beauty of working with a guy like him: plausible deniability.

"Then I don't need to know anything else." She paused momentarily. "I didn't realize you were going out of town. You have another segment on the Donnie Jones show in a few days."

"I'll only be gone a day or so. I'll be back in plenty of time."

"Good, because Stephanie might be out of commission, but we're still on mop-up duty. I'm negotiating a one-on-one with John Chase to clear the air about the video and the rumors about me. Unless you've changed your mind. You've got your new contract and your two major sponsors have offered you new deals, so skipping the interview won't hurt you financially."

"This is what we need to do to finally put this all to bed, right?" When she sighed heavily, but didn't respond, he continued. "Then that's what we're going to do."

Nate valued his privacy, but he valued his family more. Whether she believed it or not, Dray was family. He'd do whatever he needed to do to prove that to her.

* * *

Nate exited Jacksonville International Airport, picked up his rental car and drove to the home of Curtis Williams—Kendra's father.

He didn't expect to fix a decades-long problem in a single visit. But if Kendra took even the smallest step toward working things out with her father, maybe it'd go a long way toward helping him regain her trust, too.

Or maybe this was a horrible idea that would destroy everything they'd rebuilt in the past weeks.

Nate scrubbed a hand across his forehead. It was a risky move, but the payoff would be worth it.

He entered the pretty little gated community near Dutton Island and parked in the drive of the idyllic home with its covered porches spanning the width of the house on the first and second floor.

Nate rang the bell and held his breath as a shadow approached through the glass door with a colorful, geometric design.

The door opened, and the aromatic scent of spicy beef cooking wafted out to greet him. "Mr. Williams, I don't know if you remember me, but—"

"You were my daughter's *best friend*." The older man emphasized the phrase. "And the father of my grandson. Of course I know who you are." Curtis Williams folded his arms and held his gaze. "How's he coming along after his surgery?"

"Kai's doing well, sir. He loved the musical greeting card and arrangement of cookies you and your wife sent." There was an awkward pause. "May I come in?"

The man stepped aside and let him in, leading him to the living room of the spacious first floor. He invited him to have a seat.

A wave of sadness passed over the man's face. His gaze raked the floor before returning to Nate's. "Saw that nonsense on the news about her. Kendra loves Kai more than anything in the world. She ought to sue their asses for implying otherwise."

"The past week or so has been tough for her." Guilt tugged at Nate's chest. He hated that Kendra had gotten caught up in the crosshairs of the plot aimed squarely at him. "I know she'd love to hear from you."

"It's not as simple as that. Kendra is as stubborn as her mother." The old man scowled and rubbed the back of his neck. "I left her a couple of voice mails, but she hasn't returned them. I only got to speak to my grandson because Maya put him on the phone when she and the girls were visiting Kai." He eyed Nate. "Did Kendra send you?"

Nate shook his head.

"Didn't think so." He heaved a sigh, then leveled his stare at Nate again. "Then what brings you here? You asking for her hand? If so, I don't think my blessing would make much of an impression on her."

Nate scooted to the edge of his seat. "I'm here to ask you to make the effort to fix your relationship with your daughter."

Curtis raised an eyebrow. "Why do you care? You two aren't together anymore."

"I believe that your estranged relationship with Kendra is a primary reason things didn't work out with us." Nate held the man's gaze.

"You sure I'm the reason?" He poked a thumb in his chest. "I remember the report about that groupie in your room. Wasn't too long after that she left you."

"I didn't invite her to my room." Nate frowned.

"And nothing happened. Not that night or any other night while we were together."

"Still don't see what that has to do with the relationship between me and my daughter."

"Frankly, sir, you don't have a relationship. You're simply related."

"If you came here to tell me things I already know—"

"I didn't." Nate held up a hand. "I came to tell you that Kendra might act like she doesn't need you, but she does. She needs her father as much now as she did when she was a little girl."

Lines spanned the older man's forehead. His expression was weary with years of hurt and rejection. Something they had in common.

"She hated me even when she was a girl. Not at first, but between her mother and brother...she became so resentful. I wanted to set the record straight, but she was a kid. I couldn't get into all the reasons things didn't work out between her mother and me. The way she saw it, I chose my new family over her and her brother."

"Didn't you?" Nate worked to keep the accusation out of his tone, but the words dripped with it.

Curtis groaned. "No, I didn't leave Anna for Alita. Didn't even know her then. I left because I was unhappy. We both were. I wouldn't spend my life that way, like my old man did."

"I respect that, sir, but I'm sure you understand how it made your children feel. Especially Kendra. From her perspective, *she's* the reason you up and left."

"That's ridiculous." He rubbed his chin. Deep lines spanned his forehead.

"Have you told her that?"

"I've tried to show her and her brother how much I care for them. When they were younger, they'd come down and spend summers and holidays with us. As they got older, they resented being made to visit. It only made them hate me more." A pained expression accompanied the man's memories. "When they were old enough to choose, they both stopped coming. I tried giving them space, but they became more and more distant."

"I don't doubt you've tried in the past, Mr. Williams. All I'm saying is, it's worth trying again. Because if you don't, I don't know if she'll ever learn to trust any man. She'll always be afraid that the next guy is going to cheat on her or leave her."

"So you do want her back."

"I never wanted to lose her. I love her, asked her to marry me. As angry as I've been with her all these years, the truth is, I haven't met anyone I'd rather be with. I know she feels the same, but she's afraid."

"You tell her that?"

"Not in those exact words."

"Hmm…" The old man leaned forward, his hands between his knees. "Guess Kendra's not the only one who's afraid."

Nate's nostrils flared. "If I were afraid, I wouldn't be here."

"Maybe it was easier to come and talk to me than to lay it all out on the line and risk her walking away again."

Nate's gaze dropped to his hands. What the old man said was true. He hadn't been very romantic or heart-felt with Kendra. Instead, he'd pointed out that getting back together was in Kai's best interest. That line of thinking relegated Kendra to a nice bonus accessory. Something a woman like her would never stand for.

No wonder she'd turned him down. In an effort to protect his heart, he'd handled the situation poorly.

Curtis nodded knowingly, pain in his voice. "Been there. A man can only take so much, I suppose."

"You're right, Mr. Williams. My approach to Kendra was all wrong." Nate tapped the table with his forefinger. "But I'm right, too. I know she hasn't made it easy for you, but she has the right to be angry about you leaving her and Dash. She handled it badly. Maybe we're all guilty of that. But Kendra is an amazing woman. She deserves the best from both of us. It's time we both man up and give her that."

Curtis frowned at the censure, then sighed. "I convinced myself it was best just to give Kendra and Dash space and hope they came around. I guess that was just what was easiest."

"I'm having a little party this weekend to celebrate my new contract with the Marauders. I'd appreciate it if you and your wife would come. If you're willing, I'll have my assistant book your flights and hotel. Just say the word."

"I want to be the father my daughter deserves." The older man nodded. "We'll come to your party, but you don't need to pay for anything. This is something I need to do."

Nate's heart beat against his rib cage. *Mission accomplished.* Mr. Williams would make another effort to work things out with his daughter.

He'd call Kendra's mother to let her know her ex-husband would be at the party. He owed her that. On the other hand, it would be best not to tell Kendra in advance about her father's visit.

A sense of dread suddenly crept over him like kudzu vines climbing a pole.

What if Kendra resented his interference?

He heaved a sigh, releasing the tension knotting the muscles in his neck and shoulders.

Only one way to find out.

Chapter 22

Kendra dusted her face with a little powder, then applied a matte lipstick.

They'd actually pulled it off. Nate had inked his new two-year contract with the Memphis Marauders and generous deals with both his previous sponsors—a soft drink company and a rapidly growing athletic wear company poised to overtake the market within a few years. Two other sponsorships were in the works—a Memphis car dealership and a home builder based in the Carolinas.

Once Nate was ready to hang up his cleats, the sports network had already expressed interest in adding him to their parade of former players turned sports analysts.

Several months remained on her contract with Nate, but Marcus had already requested that she work with two of his other clients. The only thing that wasn't settled was her relationship with Nate.

Kendra slipped in diamond studs Nate had bought for her birthday the year he signed his first pro contract. She put on her high heel boots and a light coat, thankful the unusually cold weather had finally abated. Kai was already at Nate's, where he'd spent the night. She got in her car and swung by to pick up her mother.

Anna Williams looked lovely in a black pantsuit, her salt-and-pepper hair in pin curls, fresh from the salon. She greeted Kendra as she placed the tray of heart-shaped cookies she made for the holidays in the backseat, then got inside the car.

"Everything okay, Mama?" Kendra pulled out of her mother's small drive and headed toward the opulent beach community where Nate lived. "You're awfully quiet."

There was sadness in her mother's eyes. "You know I would never do anything to purposely hurt you or Dash?"

"Of course." A knot formed in Kendra's gut. "Why would you even have to ask?"

"Because I didn't do right by you two when it comes to your father."

"Dad made his choice when he walked away from us." Kendra's heart beat faster.

"He walked away from *me*. He loved you two. Wanted to be in your life as much as he could. It was me who made it hard for him. I was so angry. I shouldn't have talked about him the way I did in front of you kids. It made you resentful and ruined any chance of either of you having a good relationship with him."

Kendra released a long, agonizing breath. She couldn't disagree with her mother there. It was the primary reason she'd been careful to never say anything disparaging about Nate in front of their son. She didn't want him thinking ill of his dad the way she did of hers. Of course, it was easier for her. Nate hadn't been the one to walk away.

"We all make mistakes, Mama. That was a long time ago. Dash and I are adults. How we deal, or don't deal, with Dad is our choice now."

"You don't think things would've been different between you and your father if I hadn't filled your heads with the bitterness I felt toward him?" Anna's voice broke.

Kendra grimaced, her chest heavy with regret.

"I don't know. But I understand why you were so angry with him." It felt as if a weight was on her chest, compressing her lungs. "It's the same reason Nate resents me."

Her mother put a hand on her shoulder. "He was angry before, but isn't it clear how much he loves you?"

"Does he, or does he just want to keep the Johnston family tradition going?"

"Family is important to Nate, sure. But you can't honestly believe he doesn't love you. It's in his eyes when he looks at you, when he talks about you." A wistful smile broke across her mother's face. "Been there since he was a little boy. It's a special thing to have someone love you like that."

"I love him." Kendra sniffed, refusing to let the tears fall. "But I don't think things will ever be the same between us."

"I should hope not. You're both older and wiser now.

Been through the fire and come out on the other side. You'll build something stronger."

"Some part of him will always resent me, and some part of me will always be anticipating the moment he falls for a newer, shinier model." The words felt like sandpaper in her throat. "How do we get past that?"

"Forgive yourself and believe in him. It's as simple and as complicated as that." Anna's voice was firm but sympathetic. "Is giving in to your fear over what you might lose worth losing what you could have?"

Kendra pulled into the long driveway that led to Nate's beach house, not answering her mother's question. "You go ahead to the front. I'll take the tray around to the back."

Anna opened the car door and stepped out reluctantly. "Just think about what I said."

Kendra flipped down the visor mirror and gave herself a long, hard look. If only it were as simple as her mother made it sound.

She grabbed the tray and went around toward the back entrance. A light suddenly came on in a second-floor guest room. Through the sheer, gauzy curtain she could make out two figures in an embrace—Nate's twin sister Vi and Jase Hernandez.

Suddenly Vi's solo island vacation and Jase's supposed camping trip made sense. Something was going on between those two.

When Kendra looked up again, Vi was in the window staring down at her.

They were both busted.

Kendra made her way to the back door. She practically floated inside astride a warm cloud of air carrying the aroma of a variety of Southern comfort foods. Naomi's shrimp and grits, Marcus's wife Alison's chicken and dumplings, and the batch of crispy chicken Nate's youngest sister, Sydney, was frying. There was a tray of Maya's famous Cuban pork and another of her yummy empanadas.

Alison and Sydney greeted her.

Naomi, smelling of bacon and shrimp, hugged Kendra tight, then kissed her cheek. "Thank you for helping Nate through this crisis."

"It was my pleasure." Kendra smiled.

"Things didn't work out too badly for her, either," Vi interjected. "I hear Marcus has got you lined up with two more athlete clients."

"Don't start, missy." Naomi pointed a finger at her oldest daughter. "Be nice."

Vi turned to Kendra, taking the tray of cookies from her hand. "Why don't I help you put that away?"

Kendra followed Vi to a small table overflowing with desserts, including banana pudding with a perfect meringue topping and Vi's famous bourbon–brown butter pecan pie.

Vi made room for the tray of cookies, then folded her arms. She leaned closer to Kendra and lowered her voice. "Why didn't you out me in front of everyone just now?"

Kendra shrugged, removing her coat. "Figured if you wanted everyone to know you wouldn't have been sneaking around in the guest room upstairs or pretending you went to Barbados all alone."

Vi's cheeks turned crimson. She took Kendra's coat. "Walk with me while I hang this up?"

Kendra followed her to the back hall.

"Thank you." The words seemed to cause Vi physical pain. "Nate would go ballistic if he knew."

"I know, but I also know you're a grown woman and it isn't your brother's business who you're spending your vacation with…or kissing in his guest room." Kendra couldn't help the smile that tightened one side of her mouth.

Vi gave her a look that indicated she didn't appreciate her humor, which only made Kendra break out into laughter.

"This isn't funny." Vi hung her coat in the closet, then ran a hand through her box braids.

"Oh…it's serious." Kendra watched Vi's entire face flush. "Are you in love with him?"

"Don't be ridiculous." Vi folded her arms. "We're just… I don't know exactly what we're doing, but whatever it is, Nate doesn't need to know about it."

"Fine." Kendra turned to walk away.

Vi grabbed her arm. "Look, I appreciate you not ratting me out in front of my family, but this doesn't mean we're best friends."

Kendra shrugged. "Of course."

"And whether you decide to tell my brother about me and Jase or not, there's something I need to say."

Kendra folded her arms, prepared to stand her ground. "What is it?"

"Nate isn't as tough as he thinks he is. He was devastated when you walked away. I know because I was there to pick up the pieces. I won't watch my brother go through that again." There was anguish in Vi's voice.

Kendra relaxed her stance, her arms at her sides. "I didn't intend to hurt him. At the time, I thought I'd made the best decision for everyone. I was wrong. I regret that, but I can't change the past. Because of Kai, Nate and I will always be a part of each other's lives, whether you like it or not. I'd rather we be friends or at least not enemies."

Vi sighed. "I promise to take it easy on you, but you have to promise me you'll either love my brother or let him go."

"There you are." Kendra's mother came around the corner. "Just making sure you got in all right." Her gaze shifted between the two of them, then followed Vi as she returned to the kitchen. She lowered her voice. "Everything all right?"

"Nothing to worry about." She kissed her mother on the cheek.

"Good. Then I'll go and give Naomi and the girls a hand in the kitchen."

Kendra made her way into the great room. The place was overflowing with the Johnston family: Naomi and Levi; Mitchell, his wife, Monique, and their adorable infant daughter, Stella; Marcus, Alison and their two boys; Vi, Sydney and their oldest brother, Drew. The only Johnston not present was their youngest brother, Quincy, a freelance photographer on a shoot in Qatar.

Liam and Maya were caught up in an animated conversation with Monique and Mitchell—Liam's second-in-command at Pleasure Cove Luxury Resort.

Kendra sank onto the couch beside Drew and slipped her arm through his. "Thank you again for agreeing to do those interviews for the foundation. I know that went a long way in helping fix Nate's career and increasing funding."

"Glad I could help Nate for a change."

Drew's slow, crooked smile made her heart melt. He

was handsome and easily the smartest of the bunch. After an attack on his unit in Fallujah, he struggled with PTSD and had been forced to retire from the military. He often opted to stay at home or called it an early night, fearful he'd have an episode.

"You've done so much for the family, and for our country. Don't you dare think otherwise."

Drew patted her hand. "Thanks, Dray. But we should be thanking you. Without you, not sure we'd be celebrating Nate's return to the Marauders."

"My thoughts exactly, big brother." Nate stood in front of them, looking handsome enough to eat in a light blue sweater and a pair of charcoal-gray pants. He clinked a fork gently against his glass to get everyone's attention, then asked them to fill their glasses.

Nate raised his glass and turned to her with a wide smile that made her heart dance.

"To Kendra Williams, the smartest, most beautiful and most talented woman I've ever known. You've given me a chance to finish out my career with the team I love and another shot at winning it all. Most important, you've given me the best gift I could ever ask for—our son, Kai. To Kendra."

They clinked glasses and drank champagne, her heart overflowing with the love in the room and the love in Nate's eyes.

After the toast, Nate grabbed her hand and led her to his office.

"Maybe you should have a seat."

"Why, is something wrong?" She sat down, a sinking feeling in her stomach.

"Nothing's wrong." He sat beside her. "But I've invited someone here to see you."

"Who?"

Nate pushed the intercom button and asked someone to come to his office.

"Nate, what's going on? You're making me really nervous now." She studied his face, but he turned his attention to the footsteps coming down the hall and the door that slowly creaked open.

"Hello, Kendra."

"Dad? What are you doing here?" She turned to Nate, her voice lowered. "You invited him? Why?"

"Hear him out," Nate pleaded.

Kendra folded her arms. "My mother knew he was coming, didn't she?"

"I wanted to make sure she and your sister were okay with this." Nate placed a reassuring hand on hers. "We all want you to be happy, and you might not think so right now, but the state of your relationship with your father has caused a lot of pain."

She pulled her hand away. "That's my problem, Nate, not yours."

"You don't think it was my problem when you walked out because you were afraid you couldn't trust me? That it isn't Maya's problem when she won't set a date for her own wedding because of your dysfunctional relationship with your father?"

Kendra's face was hot. Each stinging accusation felt like a jab with a hot cattle prod.

"I know what I'm asking isn't easy, but it's important. To all of us." He whispered in her ear. "If something happened to your father tonight, would you be okay with how you two have left things?"

"No." The answer came without thought.

"Then talk to him. You can do this." Nate kissed her cheek. "And if you need me, I'm just down the hall."

Nate patted her father's shoulder briefly as he exited the room, closing the door behind him.

Kendra inhaled, remembering her mother's words. *He loved you...wanted to be in your life as much as he could.*

It was the very opposite of what she'd believed her entire life, no matter how hard he'd tried to convince her otherwise.

Kendra looked ahead, her eyes not meeting her father's. "So how've you been, Dad?"

Curtis Williams seemed to release a long-held breath as he sat beside her. "Physically, not too much to complain about. Mentally? It kills me that you and Dash aren't part of my life. That I hardly get to see my grandson."

Her father's voice vibrated with raw emotion. For the first time, she felt his pain. Understood that he'd been hurting, too.

She placed her warm hand on his noticeably cooler one. He clutched it as if he'd been thrown a lifeline.

It was the first time she'd let him hold her hand since she'd been old enough to cross the street alone.

"I never meant to hurt you and Dash, but I couldn't spend the rest of my life in a marriage that made your mother and me miserable. I know you don't understand—"

"As an adult, I get that, but as a kid...it was devastating." Tears rolled down her cheeks and she wiped at them angrily. "It was hard enough knowing that you'd left us. But what hurt most is I couldn't understand why you didn't love me and Dash enough to stay, but you chose to stay with Maya and Cole and their mom."

"Don't ever think I didn't love you and your brother." He squeezed her hand. "Walking away from my little boy and my baby girl was one of the hardest things I've ever done."

"Then why'd you do it?"

Her father sighed. "Because I didn't want you to grow up the way I did. With parents who resented the hell out of each other. In a house filled with anger and tension and constant arguing. I lived through that, and I didn't want it for you and Dash."

"Why didn't you ever tell us that? All this time, I kept thinking that there must've been something about me that drove you away."

"Kendra, I'm sorry I made you feel that way. I never meant to hurt you and Dash. I only wanted to protect you. Instead, I lost you both."

"It was hard watching you be the perfect father to Maya and Cole. All I could think about was all the times you weren't there for me. It hurt too much to be there and pretend everything was okay. It was easier to hold onto the resentment. So I did. And when I pulled away from you, you didn't put up a fight. That only made me angrier."

Her father shook his head. "I kept telling myself that you and your brother just needed a little space and then you'd come around. The truth is, I was hurt by your rejection, and it was easier not to deal with it. For that, I'm truly sorry. But know this…not a single day has gone by that I haven't thought of you and your brother, hoping we could one day be a family again."

"I believe you, Dad." She accepted the handkerchief

her father offered and wiped the tears from her cheeks. "I'm sorry I pushed you away."

He held her in his arms. "Sorry I put you and Dash in a position where you felt you had to choose between your mother and me. I should've handled it better."

"Me, too," Kendra mumbled against her dad's chest. She missed the smell of his cologne.

He squeezed her shoulder. "I can't make up for how I've hurt you in the past, but I'd like to build a relationship with you now. We've already lost so much time."

Kendra found comfort in her father's embrace. One conversation wouldn't instantly heal the deep wounds they'd inflicted on each other. But it was a start, and she had Nate to thank for it.

Chapter 23

Everyone had gone home and Kai was asleep in his bed. They'd had a wonderful night, celebrating with family and a handful of his teammates. But now it was nice to have the house all to themselves.

"Thank you, Nate, for what you did today for me and my dad." Kendra sat beside him on the sofa in the den. "We had a really good talk today, and we're both determined to work on building our relationship."

"That's great, Dray." He squeezed her hand, genuinely happy for them both.

"My dad said something tonight before he and Alita left. He said he was sorry that he was the reason I had trouble trusting people, and that he hoped I'd learn to trust the people in my life who love me. He was talking about you, wasn't he? That's why you arranged this."

"Yes." Nate threaded his fingers through hers, his throat suddenly dry. He turned his body toward hers. "Kendra, I care about you…no…" He released a deep sigh and raised his eyes to hers, his pulse racing. "I love you, and I need you in my life."

She stared at him, wide-eyed. His declaration had taken her by surprise. "We've been through so much these past few weeks, Nate. Experiences like that can make you extremely emotional."

"I know." His breathing was slow and measured. "And despite the crazy ups and downs, I haven't been this happy in a long time. I want you and Kai in my life every day. That's what makes me happy."

"I care about you, Nate. I want us to be a family, too. But you need to be sure about your feelings. That you truly want to be with me, and not just because I'm Kai's mom."

"The way I feel about you… It isn't just because we have a son together. It's because you're still that girl I fell in love with at the roller-skating rink all those years ago. The best friend I shared my feelings with when they were too raw to share with anyone else."

He pressed a hand to her cheek and smiled. "You are the *only* woman I've ever truly loved. The woman I want to wake up to every morning. The one I want to cook dinners with. The person I want to dance to old-school jams with until I'm eighty."

She laughed as she blinked back tears.

Nate smiled. "Being with you these past few weeks, I've come to realize how incomplete my life is without you. I miss my best friend, the woman I have so much history with. The woman I want to build my future with."

"I love you, too, Nate, and I want to be with you, but I also want my career. I shouldn't have to choose."

"No, you shouldn't. I was wrong to ask you to do that before. I was so busy trying to give you the life I thought you deserved that I didn't stop to listen to what you actually wanted. I won't make that mistake again. I promise you, I'm going to support your career, just like you've always supported mine."

Kendra grinned, leaning into him. She pressed her mouth to his and gave him a slow, lingering kiss that made heat rise in his chest and his pulse race.

"One last thing." She locked her gaze with his. "Now that we've laid all our cards on the table, we wipe the slate clean. No more apologies, no more guilt. I love you and I trust you to be the man that Kai and I need. One day, I hope you'll be able to trust me, too. That I won't walk away from you or hurt you."

He cupped her cheek and kissed her softly on the lips. "I do trust you. I trust that if an issue ever rises again, that you'll come and talk to me so we can work it out together."

"I promise." She nodded, kissing him again.

Nate held her tight, his heart overflowing with joy and contentment.

His life was good.

He had his family, a generous new contract and lucrative endorsement deals that would allow him to continue supporting the people and causes he cared about.

Still, there was one prize that eluded Nate. He'd do

everything in his power to help the Marauders win the big one and walk away champions.

But nothing—not even a championship ring—could make him happier than he was right now.

* * * * *

SPECIAL EXCERPT FROM

##
HARLEQUIN®

Rafe Lawson is only driven by his music and living a life away from the influence of his powerful father. The woman he meets at a high-profile celebration won't change his playboy ways. Still, Rafe is intrigued by the stunning secret service agent who never mixes business and pleasure. He has no choice but use his legendary Lawson power of seduction to win over Avery Richards…

Read on for a sneak peek at
SURRENDER TO ME,
the next exciting installment in author Donna Hill's
THE LAWSONS OF LOUISIANA series!

He'd noticed her the moment she walked in, and it was clear, even in an eye-popping black gown, that she was there as more than an invited guest. He could tell by the way her gaze covertly scanned the room, noted the exits and followed at a discreet distance from the vice president that she was part of his security detail—secret service. He had an image of a .22 strapped to her inner thigh.

Unlike many highbrow gatherings of politicos and the like that were too reserved for Rafe's taste, a Lawson party was the real deal. Full of loud laughter, louder conversations and the music to go with it. So of course he had to get particularly close to talk to her.

He gave her time to assess the layout before he approached. He came alongside her. "Can I get you anything?"

KPEXP0717

She turned cinnamon-brown eyes on him, fanned by long, curved lashes. Her smile was practiced, distant, but Rafe didn't miss the rapid beat of her pulse in the dip of her throat that belied her cool exterior. Her sleek right brow rose in question as she took him in with one long glance.

"Clearly you're not one of the waitstaff," she said with a hint of amusement in her voice.

"Rafe Lawson."

Her eyes widened for a split second. "Oh, the scandalous one."

He pressed his hand to his chest dramatically. "Guilty as charged, cher, but I have perfectly reasonable explanations for everything."

Her eyes sparkled when the light hit them. "I'm sure you do, Mr. Lawson."

"So what can I get for you that won't interfere with you being on duty?"

She tensed ever so slightly.

"Trust me. I've grown up in this life. I can spot secret service a mile away. Although I must admit that you bring class to the dark suits and sunglasses."

She glanced past him to where her colleague stood near the vice president. In one fluid motion she gave a barely imperceptible lift of her chin, a quick scan of the room and said, "Nice to meet you," as she made a move to leave.

He held her bare arm. "Tell me your name," he commanded almost in her ear. He inhaled her, felt the slight shiver that gripped her.

"Avery."

Rafe released her and followed the dangerously low-cut back of her dress with his gaze until she was out of sight.

Don't miss SURRENDER TO ME
by Donna Hill, available August 2017
wherever Harlequin® Kimani Romance™
books and ebooks are sold.

Get 2 Free Books,
Plus 2 Free Gifts—
just for trying the
Reader Service!

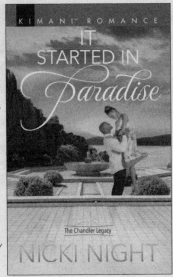

Earn points from all your Harlequin book purchases from wherever you shop.

Turn your points into **FREE BOOKS** of your choice
OR
EXCLUSIVE GIFTS from your favorite authors or series.

Join for FREE today at
www.HarlequinMyRewards.com.

Harlequin My Rewards is a free program (no fees) without any commitments or obligations.

MYR17

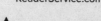